CHRISTOPHER

Caribbean
Writers
Series

GEOFFREY DRAYTON

D0081940

CARIBBEAN WRITERS SERIES
Editorial Adviser: Professor John Figueroa

6

Christopher

CARIBBEAN WRITERS SERIES

GEOFFREY DRAYTON

Christopher

Introduction by Louis James
University of Kent at Canterbury

HEINEMANN
LONDON

Heinemann Educational Books Ltd
48 Charles Street, London W1X 8AH
P.M.B. 5205, Ibadan · P.O. BOX 25080, Nairobi
EDINBURGH · MELBOURNE · TORONTO · AUCKLAND
HONG KONG · SINGAPORE · KUALA LUMPUR
NEW DELHI

ISBN 0 435 98235 4

© Geoffrey Drayton 1959
© Introduction Louis James 1972
First published by William Collins Ltd 1959
First published in Caribbean Writers Series 1972

To
RICHARD & DAPHNE
BANCROFT

Printed Offset Litho and bound in Great Britain
by Cox & Wyman Ltd,
London, Fakenham and Reading

INTRODUCTION

By Louis James

University of Kent at Canterbury
Formerly University College of the West Indies

Christopher (1959) is one of a small but important group of West Indian novels about childhood that includes George Lamming's *In the Castle of my Skin* (1953) and Michael Anthony's *The Year in San Fernando* (1965). The central place children hold in Caribbean communities is reflected in the quality of perception West Indian writers often bring to their accounts of the child's world. Further, since the child's vision is by definition free from many of the adult preconceptions that distort the writer's awareness, the literature of childhood has played a significant part in the cultural self-discovery that the Caribbean literary movement of the last few decades has shown. One remembers the importance of Twain's *Huckleberry Finn* in the creation of an American literature. Each child discovers his world afresh; Geoffrey Drayton's Christopher plays Columbus.

Like Lamming's better-known *In the Castle of my Skin* Drayton's novel is set in Barbados, but while Lamming's hero is one of the black peasant class, Christopher is of a white planter family. Each shows life on different sides of the plantation wall, and the two views provide interesting complements to each other. Both books also are poetic rather than conventionally novelistic. Events do happen in *Christopher*: The boy grows up, moves from one school to another, learns to paint and matures physically. Meanwhile Gip, his black nurse, ages and dies. His mother has a stillborn son. Yet to look for a firm pattern of events is to invite frustration. Indeed, the clock-time of events is secondary to the unbroken inner time of Christopher's consciousness as it moves towards the point of independence at which it is no longer a child's. It is interesting to note that Geoffrey Drayton originally wrote the novel in three sections: childhood in Barbados, further education in England, and return to the island. Teaching in England after graduation from Cambridge in 1952, however, his observation of the psychology of sensitive only children in particular, lead to a change of plan. The second section was never published, and the third was used for a B.B.C. talk, 'Return to the Island' (reprinted in *The Listener*, March 15, 1962). Meanwhile the boy's development over two decades was telescoped back into a tight psychological unity framed by place and three dominating human relationships.

The compression is not without weaknesses. There is uncertainty about the boy's age at any particular time in the novel, which, if known, would help the reader evaluate Christopher's reactions better. Although the book is intimately concerned with plants and flowers, we do not have the sense of seasonal cycle that underpins Anthony's *The Year in San Fernando*. There are glimpses of the boy's life which are not unified into the character Drayton gives us— for example Christopher with his Uncle Francis wanting to be a doctor. These limitations, however, do not destroy the novel's strong recreation of a child's developing awareness.

In Christopher's world, with the exception of the black nurse, Gip, places and things are more important than people. Looking down on a Bridgetown street: "People", Christopher thought as he watched the patterns of moving brightness, "are not interesting, like things . . . Neither the sounds they made nor the colours they borrowed were as attractive as the sound of trees or the colours of plants." (p. 59.) Flowers are more tractable to his poetic imagination. He can distinguish coreopsis and calendulas before he can understand the insecurity behind his father's vicious moods. Shut out from the sexual knowledge of the village boys, he retreats into a secret knowledge of how to grow snails from eggs and the way to transplant ferns. A centre of his world is his private garden with its beds laid in pieces of truck tyre. He shares with plants an instinctive feeling for a good growing atmosphere—for the dried-up pond jungled with bananas, for the centre of the orchard, and the cliff hollow by the pond where the family pets are buried. There is

menace as well as beauty in this world; there are harmless
lizards with legs, silver snakes that bite, and forty-leg cater-
pillars that sting in the dark, while the pond with its lilies
hides an unseen monster that destroys ducks and their eggs.
As he grows up, Christopher's passion for nature is internalised into art. The colours and forms that haunt him take
shape in his paintings, and anger and emotional awakening
so glow from his book that his mother seeing them turns the
pages quicker, herself disturbed.

Yet nature for Christopher is not as independent of people
as at first appears. Gip in particular gives the boy the will to
live that informs his joy in things: as Christopher's mother
wistfully realises, Gip "had made the colours of his day;
and her life had not left his when she put out the lamp at
night". (p. 189.) When Christopher is dangerously ill, it is
only Gip who can heal him, staying with him through the
night in a cot at the foot of the bed. Through Gip, too,
Christopher comes into touch with the black community. It
is not only that native infusions help him when he is ill; the
black world of devout faith and of obeah, of drums heard
by moonlight and sexual hieroglyphs etched on agave leaves
form an important part of his imagination.

Yet since Christopher must remain outside the black community because of his colour and status, what he gains from
it is fragmented and destructive. He is fascinated by native
superstition, terrifying himself when his childish wish for the
power of obeah seems to have gone murderously awry. But
on the other hand he cannot know the villagers' acceptance
of the natural world.

> By nature Christopher would have tended to think of
> light and darkness as the Negroes did—as the opening
> and shutting of an eye; but his upbringing had estranged
> his nature, so that, until now, he had regarded the sun
> rather as a lamp, lighted, like the oil lamps and storm
> lanterns at home, to bring respite from the shadows, the
> dreams and the fright. (pp. 56–57.)

Gyp is both one of the black community and one who by
her devout religion and position as nurse to the Stevens
reinforces moral prohibitions against the freedoms of her

group. For instance: "According to Gip, it was wicked to be
naked—probably even under water. The fact that the
Negro boys in the tenantry bathed at the standpipe without
any clothes at all . . . merely proved that he shouldn't."
(p. 178.)

Tensions underlie the relation between the black and
white worlds, unobtrusive though erupting at moments of
stress. A maid, being diffidently dismissed by Mrs. Stevens,
explodes: "You white people think we ain't got no pride,
that you can pick us up and push us back when and how it
suit you." (p. 102.) The effects of exploitation emerge
before the terrified Christopher as a beggar running with
sores, peering into the shiny car, menacing him says:
"Spent it all didja? Well, do you know where you got it all
to spend? From bastards like me, slaving from first of
January to last of December for you friggers . . ." (p. 61.)
The social position of Gip, provokes Christopher to ask:
"What does it mean . . . when somebody's better than somebody else?" (p. 47.)

The most destructive tensions for Christopher, however,
come not from the black-white confrontation, but from
tensions within the white community itself. On his father's
side lies the old plantocracy, hit by falling sugar prices after
the war, facing comparative poverty. On his mother's side,
however, he is related to the merchant class who made
fortunes in the same period and in the same upheaval. His
maternal grandfather, Mr. Fraser, was a small-trader of
somewhat dubious background who now owns a spacious
new house and is chauffeured in a hired car. So Christopher
as the visible issue of the family connection becomes the
focus of double resentments—of the Frasers' jealousy of the
Stevens' better class, and of the Stevens' hatred of the
traders' newly gained wealth, especially as no help is
offered to the planter's family when in need. The affectionate but weak mother can do little to protect her son, and
ironically the father's enmity is intensified because Christopher has so much of his own sensitive, obstinate blood.

The novel is about the way Christopher moves through
the tensions within and around him. Each section of the
book is named after a person—the figure in Christopher's

8

life from whom he is becoming independent. Freedom from his father comes when he sees in his father's eyes the hate that distorted those of the beggar outside his grandfather's car, and he can then await his father's flogging with a cruel mixture of understanding and rejection. His closest tie with his mother is ironically brought about by guilt lest his attempt to put obeah on the new cook has indirectly caused the stillbirth of his baby brother; it is broken when she sets his fears at rest. It is not she who holds Christopher back from jumping into the grave after Gip when she dies, either physically or metaphorically. Christopher's relationship with Gip is different again: her hold on him loosens in the natural process of growing up. She continues to dream of the young child she once nursed, while Christopher matures, but even so her reassuring presence becomes absorbed into Christopher's personality, internalised. Before the final scene of Gip's funeral we see Christopher waking up in the moonlit night. He feels fear: "But was all right. She was still there, sitting peacefully in the rocking-chair. There was nothing to be afraid of." (p. 188.) Yet Gip is dead.

As a novel, *Christopher* has the limitations of its hero's own vision. Characterisation apart from that of the boy, and the structure of event and circumstance, tends to be weak. This is particularly true of the black characters—even Gip does not have the solidity her importance in the novel demands. The book's strengths are those of poetry. It is delicately evocative, while at the same time remaining precise. Drayton gives us the aura of Christopher's plantation home, yet the book could also serve as a map to someone visiting the area in Barbados where it is based. Flowers and trees create the atmosphere of the book—they are named lace-plants, field-crocus, golden rod, alamander, calendulas, coreopsis, cordia trees, casuarinas, chili-plum trees: yet at the same time they are a poetic part of the boy's world. At points in his life they also unobtrusively underline his development. The early chapters are redolent with fern, uncurling their delicate fiddle-heads in the damp air. As he moves towards sexual awareness, we see the obscene graffiti on spiky agave leaves in the dark gully. When Gip dies, Christopher sees for the first time the weird scentless beauty of the Fairmont orchid house; and for Gip's funeral he strips the garden of its blooms. The book is at once a picture of a boy growing up, and the evocation of an atmosphere recognisably Barbadian.

Besides *Christopher*, Geoffrey Drayton has written a variety of stories and poems. These have appeared mainly in *Bim* and on the B.B.C. programme *Caribbean Voices*. The first section of *Christopher*, 'The Father', was published in *Bim* (Vol. 7, No. 26, January–June 1958, pp. 92–118). His best known short story is probably 'Mr. Dombey the Zombie', first broadcast on the B.B.C., and reprinted by Andrew Salkey in *West Indian Stories* (Faber, London, 1960). It is a piece of grimly whimsical fantasy quite unlike *Christopher*. *Three Meridians*, a slim volume of his verse, was published in 1950 by the Ryerson Press, Canada, and in 1961 Secker & Warburg, London, published his novel of witchcraft in Spain, *Zohara*. At the moment Mr. Drayton is Project Director for the Oil Department of the *Economist* Intelligence Unit.

Louis James

GLOSSARY

auroras: small sea shells
Berbice chair: wooden easy chair with extended arms that serve as foot-rests
forty-legs: mildly poisonous centipedes
green peas: sea shells
Man-the-canes: game of robbers in ambush
puppies' eyes: sea shells
sea egg: edible sea urchin with short, stiff spikes
sucks: drains
thousands: minnows

Part One : The Father

1

THEY PLAYED together under the trees, the solemn child and the lizards. The lizards showed yellow tongues when they chased one another, and were far greener than the banana leaves they rested on. There were other lizards too, some so transparent and swift that he never saw them unless he pretended to be asleep. One kind had no legs, and moved like silver lightning where the dead leaves collected in the orchard-bottom and rotted. He hated these. They reminded him, in their movements, of the congers he had seen in the reef pools when the tide was out. Always the congers had slithered forward, under the rock where he was standing, so that he had been afraid of going on. Besides, Gip, his nurse, had said that the shiny lizards would bite, and were poisonous. He pretended they didn't exist; and when he went into the orchard-bottom he wore shoes, just as his uncle, who hunted lions in Kenya, wore puttees and boots to protect himself from snake-bite.

The banana trees had been planted in circles around a dried-up pond. The centre of the pond was still muddy, and the leaves there greener and glossier than anywhere else. Gip didn't like him to go down that far. His shoes got dirty, and she had to clean them. If, too, he was having a successful hunt and did not come when she called, she couldn't follow him without sinking up to her ankles in mud. She was large and heavy—like a rhinoceros perhaps. Sometimes, when he was feeling naughty, he would shoot a mud ball at her, hoping she would stop suddenly, and fall on crumpled legs. This is what the rhinoceros always did—or so his uncle had told him.

Today the sun was especially hot. The lizards moved lazily; and since he was not interested in killing them, only in chasing them and taking wild shots with his catapult, the game began to pall. He climbed up the bank and woke Gip.

" Tell me about the obeah-woman," he said.

Gip stirred. She looked cool and comfortable, with a white apron spread over her ample lap. Christopher leant against her legs until she lifted him up.

" Your mammie say I'se not to tell you nothing more 'bout obeah. You going to have bad dreams to-night and wake everybody up."

Christopher frowned. They really couldn't be helped, his bad dreams, and had nothing to do, he was sure, with the obeah-woman. Anyhow the sun was shining.

" Why do they die," he asked, " when they find a white feather in a bottle? "

" Because they don't know no better. They don't go to church like you and me."

" Nat went to church. I've seen him there."

" Nat was a silly, good-for-nothing old man," she told him vehemently. " He went from the church door to the obeah-woman. You got to believe in one thing or the other."

" Daddy says if you don't believe in the obeah-woman she can't hurt you."

" What your pappie know 'bout obeah? He better talk things he know."

Gip saw a little smile gather around Christopher's mouth. If he hadn't been so young she would have given him credit for baiting her; but he was too young, she thought, to know anything of the intolerance with which she regarded her employer. She continued hurriedly nevertheless.

" I tell you 'bout the cholera."

Christopher settled himself more comfortably.

" I was only a little girl at the time."

" How old? "

" Oh, six or seven," she said; " and that was long time ago. Doctors them days didn't know nothing 'bout medicines—except castor oil and eucalyptus. They didn't know nothing 'bout cholera at any rate. Some said to drink a lot of water if you felt it coming on; but for sure the cholera was in the water. People died like flies, black people that is—it didn't seem to trouble the whites—and the government had to send around a cart to collect them. They buried them all together in a big hole . . ."

" Where? " Christopher asked.

Actually he knew the story by heart, but he liked to insert questions as often as possible in order to postpone the really interesting part.

But all too quickly Gip began to relate how her family had taken the cholera. Her father had died, and then her brother. When her brother died, she had, by mistake, been put in the cart with him and the other corpses. She woke up soon after, and started to scream. The driver left his cart and ran, thinking a duppy was after him. She had had to climb out and find her way home.

" What was it like with the dead people? " Christopher was determined not to let the subject end, even if the story had.

" I don't rightly remember. I didn't stay long enough to find out. They was cold, I expect. Dead people always cold."

" Did they smell? " he asked.

" Lord! Master Chris, what awful things you do say."

" Did they? " he persisted. " I don't mean the smell black people always have, but like things that die."

" No! Of course they didn't smell like that. They was only just dead."

" Would they, after a long time, though? " But he did not wait to have that answered. " What happened to the rat," he asked, " that died under my floor? "

" The ants might have eaten him," Gip suggested.

" And do ants eat us after we are dead? Will they eat Grannie Stevens? " There was a note of enthusiasm about the second question.

" I do believe your grannie's right. You are a horrible small boy."

" Well," he brushed that aside, " I hope they do. I don't like Grannie Stevens. When she comes to stay she won't let me have the chips Bessie cuts off her dresses."

" What you want them chips for? They's black and ugly."

" My snails hatch best on black cloth. They think they're still on the ground. If I put them on white cloth the eggs go bad."

" Put them on coloured cloth then, the chips off your mammie's dresses."

" That's silly. Who ever heard of snails on coloured cloth! Besides, I want those for my books. And I don't want white ones, and I don't want black ones in my books. I don't want white ones at all," he concluded in a forthright fashion, and climbed down.

Grown-ups, even Gip, were really most stupid, he decided, as he marched off to look for more snails' eggs. The snails were alive inside their shells and could easily see what kind of cloth lay under them. If the cloth was white they just curled themselves up, turned black, and died. They smelt awful when they died.

As for the coloured bits of material, these he stuck side by side on large sheets of newspaper. Where they didn't quite meet one another he crayoned the paper between. He almost had enough of these sheets to cover the whole floor of his bedroom. When he did he would get several bottles of glue, pour them all over the floor, and make himself a carpet—a much prettier carpet than the one in the drawing-room, which was black and white and orangey. His carpet would be of all colours, and not have the same pattern anywhere.

The ferneries were the best place to look for snails' eggs. He was not supposed to go into them. Joe, the gardener, was fierce on this point.

" Can't grow ferns," he had complained, " when Master Chris breaks all the young shoots looking for snails, or cuts them off to feed them. Who ever heard of feeding snails anyway? "

Joe wasn't very well educated. He couldn't even read. Certainly he knew nothing about snails.

But Joe had had his way, and Christopher now entered the ferneries over the wall, through the latticed and creeper-covered roof. This was actually more exciting. It also involved disturbing the creeper in places where hands could not easily reach. The lushest water-lemons had come to light in those spots.

So far no damaged fern-shoots had betrayed Christopher's continued visits to the fernery; nor did he any longer pick them as snail-food. With a little extra effort he could collect enough sprouts from the wild maidenhair that grew in the crevices of the orchard walls. He had compared the two varieties, the wild and the cultivated, by tasting one of each. Apart from a slightly saltier taste in the wild kind there was no difference—and the young snails had not suffered either.

To-day, as usual, he stuffed his pockets with ripe water-lemons, and climbed carefully down. The ferns were at their best just now, after the rains. They were ranged in huge pots along terraces of white limestone. The pots and the limestone were mossed over, and wild maidenhair covered everything except the paths. From the roof hung baskets with more ferns, and orchids; here and there the rich green was slashed with the reds of single impatiens. A couple of anthuriums stuck up pollen-coated fingers. They had no smell, and looked hard and unfriendly, as if covered all over with candle-wax.

Christopher was in no hurry. He dipped his hand in the lily-pool to watch the mosquito-fish. They came quite close to the surface, sniffed his hand, and darted away again.

Just then he heard footsteps crunching on the gravel path outside the fernery. He recognised his mother's voice. The other voice was throaty like a man's. It belonged to the fat lady with four fingers who grew roses. She had lost a finger when a rose thorn stuck it. Christopher prayed that they would pass; but he knew they wouldn't. The fat lady grew anthuriums as well as roses and liked to gloat over her better specimens. He scuttled into the darkest part of the fernery and hid behind a plant with giant fronds. Mrs. Stevens unlatched the door and pushed it open. The fat lady was talking.

" I don't really like the green ones. But they are awfully rare. And so huge! I had one the other day as big as a soup-plate. Now the orange ones—I see you haven't an orange one—they're another matter. Small, but such a wonderful colour . . ."

Christopher did not listen. He never felt at ease with Mrs. Williams. He was afraid of her four fingers and hard voice. His mother was not listening either. She had stopped to look at something; and now her weak eyes were searching the shadows. She interrupted Mrs. Williams in the midst of a continuous chatter about various species of anthurium.

" I wonder where Christopher is," she said loudly. " He can't know you are here or he'd have come to speak."

Christopher watched his mother. He did not know

what she had been looking at on the ground but interpreted her remark as an invitation to come out of
hiding if he was there. He held his breath until, pre-
sently, the pair went away. Their voices faded in the
direction of the orchard. The door had been left open.

When he came from behind his pot of giant ferns
Christopher was horrified to find that in his hurry to
escape he had brushed against and bruised several
shoots. Now Joe would know! He tried to mend the
shoots; but on so warm a day they were already limp.
He broke them off and threw them away. Then,
remembering that his mother had gone to look for him
in the orchard, he ran after her.

He arrived, panting, just as she was asking Gip his
whereabouts.

" Oh, here he is," Mrs. Williams bellowed, in her
hearty attempt at friendliness, " looking very hot. What
have you been doing, Christopher? Why didn't you
come and say hallo to me? "

" Finding snails' eggs," he told her.

" In the fernery, I bet," Mrs. Stevens said; but she
spoke casually, as if afraid to make the words into a
question.

" You don't put them in your pockets? " the fat
woman exclaimed, pointing a horrified finger at his
bulging trousers.

Unwillingly Christopher produced the water-lemons.
He was sure now that his mother would know; but he
hoped she would not tell his father. He offered the
fruit.

" No. Water-lemons I found. Would you like one? "

Mrs. Williams helped herself. He offered the other

to his mother. She was looking at him with eyes wide in sudden alarm.

" How did you get into the fernery? " she cried. " Not through the roof? "

Christopher said nothing. But he realised that if his mother was frightened she might tell on him to prevent his doing it again.

" Oh, it's quite easy," he explained carelessly. " I hold on till my feet are on the top ledge."

Mrs. Stevens was not at all relieved.

" Those beams are rotten as sawdust," she told him angrily. " You might have broken your neck."

" I haven't yet," he answered, somewhat petulantly —and knew at once this was the wrong thing to have said. He became annoyed with himself, more annoyed because he felt tears start to his eyes—and his mother and Mrs. Williams merely stood and stared, waiting for him to continue. He hated them standing there, staring with accusation. " And I don't care if I do break my neck," he exploded finally.

He turned away and ran down the slope to the banana trees and the fat, friendly green lizards.

Mrs. Stevens spoke briefly to Gip and started back towards the house. She walked in front of her guest, abstractedly, as if she would have preferred to be going in the other direction, after Christopher. Mrs. Williams was laughing.

" Thank heavens I don't have any small children. Hens are bad enough—always nesting in the gardens and sitting on the seedlings."

Christopher told himself that he hated Mrs. Williams. He did not like anyone at this point, not even Gip.

19

2

THE FERNERY INCIDENT was closed. Actually Mrs.
Stevens had not told her husband. Joe had.

" Master Chris been breaking off fern-shoots again,"
he had complained, " feeding snails."

Mr. Stevens had not listened to Christopher's
attempted explanation. Christopher had never been
any good at explaining things to his father; recently he
had given up trying. Instead his eyes creased to
stubborn slits, his nostrils flared, and with some un-
governed remark that sounded familiarly like arrogance
he would infuriate his questioner. The result was usually
a verdict without a judgment.

The verdict this time was severe. Christopher was
not to be allowed to keep snails' eggs in future. Gip was
informed. She said nothing. A look of amazement slid
across her face and hardened. She turned away
and went to look for Christopher. She did not find
him.

Christopher was hiding in the triangular-shaped
garden that was his own. The flower-beds in this garden
were made of old truck rims filled with soil. They were
set well apart and wild flowers had been planted in the
spaces between, old maid's bush and field-crocus,

golden rod, lilies and lace-plants—whatever had taken Christopher's fancy. At the apex of the triangle a thumbergia grew luxuriantly. It overflowed on all sides and climbed up the wall behind. Under the broad pads of leaves and the cascades of purple was a small dark place, where the creeper lifted to the wall. Christopher had hidden himself there. He heard Gip come by and call; but he did not answer.

He was angry with his mother. Why hadn't she told his father how the fern-shoots came to be broken? If she hadn't frightened him into hiding, no damage would have been done. He had been using the fernery for a long time now and no fiddles had suffered.

His anger was spacious and ill-defined. Underneath it he was vaguely aware of being in the wrong. But he had been punished; and he wished to punish someone in return. His mother was the most vulnerable.

He was angry too with Gip. He wanted to be comforted by her; but she wasn't even looking for him properly. They didn't really love him at all. He wished a centipede would bite him. Gip had told him that centipedes hid in the moist dark places in the gardens—under the thumbergia for instance. If a centipede bit him, perhaps he would die. At least he would be very ill; and then they would be sorry. His eyes grew hot at the thought of how sorry they would be.

But it was very boring sitting under the thumbergia, especially when nobody was searching for him. He decided to go and collect cow dung for his lilies. He crept out, took trolley and fork, and went towards the pond. Nobody saw him go—which was all the better.

Perhaps they would think he had run away. He went over the slope. The cows moved aside as he pushed carelessly among them.

There is an art in collecting cow dung for packing lilies. A two-pronged fork is essential equipment. You spear a lump where it has splashed into a thin round cake, and lift. If the lump does not come away clean and whole, the dung is too recent; it has not been weathered long enough by the sun, and will be too strong for the lily bulbs.

Christopher filled his trolley and wheeled it back to the garden. Occasionally it overturned and he had to stop and reload. Once in the garden he piled the lumps on an empty bed and began to break them into pieces.

The supper bell rang before he was finished. He would be late, he decided. Anger had left him, but resentment made him casual of further sin and he was purposely slow in washing. The goldfish in the tank darted at the flecks of dung that floated off his hands. He dried the palms on the seat of his trousers, noticed that the nails were clean—he had bitten them so short that nothing could collect under them—and walked determinedly up the front steps.

His parents were already seated. Cinder had served the soup. Christopher mumbled an excuse and took his place beside his mother. Mr. Stevens sat at the head of the long mahogany table, with his wife and Christopher on the left. Coreopses stood in a bowl in the centre, dropping yellow dust around themselves. There was no conversation till the soup had been cleared away. Then Mrs. Stevens spoke.

" What have you done all afternoon? " she asked.

" Cow-dunged," he said briefly, refusing to be mollified by her soft voice and interest.

" Did you wash your hands properly? " his father asked.

" Yes, sir," and he held them up, keeping his eyes fixed on the coreopses. Mr. Stevens must have been satisfied because he began to talk of something else. Christopher was not included in the conversation, for which he was grateful. He day-dreamed through the rest of the meal; once, when Cinder stopped behind him and turned down his shirt-collar, he pretended not to notice.

The meal finished. His parents returned to the verandah. Beetles were beginning to fly in through the door; Cinder closed it, but they came in through the open window. Boodles chased them hungrily while waiting for her dinner. Christopher gave instructions as Cinder cut up fish on a tin plate. She had a habit of giving Boodles too many vegetables—which the cat never ate—and not enough fish or meat. As she passed the plate over, Cinder grinned at him and ruffled his hair.

Boodles ran in and out in Christopher's legs as he carried the food down the corridor and put it in a corner. He waited till she had eaten the fish and stretched her long white length with satisfaction. When first he had been given Boodles, he used to leave the scraps in case she returned later to finish them. But his father had complained that this attracted cock-roaches. Now, if Boodles was hungry at night, she had to fare for herself. She always went to sleep at the

23

bottom of Christopher's bed; but if he woke during the night she was never there. He presumed she went off to hunt lizards or sleeping birds. He would have preferred her not to catch birds—in fact, she was spanked when he did catch her at it; but she had never learnt. The spanking was therefore administered tenderly. Boodles did not know when she was being naughty, just as, very often, he did not know either.

He gave the scraps to one of the alsatians that was nosing around outside the kitchen door, and returned to his dung pile.

Even at this time of year the nights came quickly. One moment the sky seemed stitched with luminous patches and the next it was a monotonous purple. Now the evening grows momentarily silent. A bull-frog calls gutturally in the distance and the silence ends. All the whistling frogs sing together, irritatingly at first, and then becoming part of another kind of silence. Through it you can hear the negro boys in the village a mile away, screaming as they play Man-in-the-canes or some such game.

Gip came to fetch Christopher for his bath and bed. He pleaded for a few more minutes.

" The night dews will give you a cold," she fussed— and stood watching a while. Christopher's actions were precise and unhurried, like his speech. She laughed gently to herself, gently and a little grimly. If only he weren't so much like his father, she thought; maybe they'd get on better.

" Will you read to-night? " Christopher asked, giving her a dungy hand.

" You and your reading," she complained. " You'll

have me blind before my time, reading by that old oil lamp. And who'll look after me then? "

" I will of course." He spoke spontaneously, without attempt to ingratiate.

" You'll have your mother to look after. That'll be plenty."

" Will I? " The excitement was momentary. " But Daddy'll do that."

" Maybe you'll have your daddy too. He's a whole lot older than the mistress."

" How much older? "

" That I ain't sure about—ten fifteen years maybe."

" Is daddy as old as Grandfather? "

" Good Lord, no! Your grandpa must be old as me."

" But you're not really old, are you? Grandfather has wrinkles all over, and his hands are blue in places. You don't use a stick to walk with either. Grandfather is about a hundred. Every time he comes he gives me a penny and says it may be the last. Do you think he's going to die soon? " He spoke in a hushed tone, partly because the thought frightened him, partly because they had entered the house. His parents out on the verandah could not hear anything that was being said at the back of the house; but, even so, his father did not seem to like his asking questions about his mother's family. Christopher could not imagine why. Gip said that it wasn't true, that it was only because Mr. Stevens had once worked for his grandfather and people sometimes disagreed with those they worked for. But personally, he thought that it was because Grannie Stevens was such a selfish old woman, whereas his other grandmother laughed and petted him; and Granddad

Fraser gave him pennies—or shillings, as Gip insisted on calling them. Penny was a much nicer word than shilling—and, as far as he was concerned, it made no difference; all coins went into a red tin in the safe by his father's bed. They bought him presents at Christmas, he had been told. He would have preferred to have the pennies to shoot tiddly-winks. Presents at Christmas were always shirts or handkerchiefs or trousers—nothing he could play with.

The shower was cold, as usual. He felt it with his toe, pranced around yelling, and finally plunged under. He would have liked to bath at midday when the sun overhead had warmed the tanks. At sunset the water grew cool with the wind.

Gip gathered him into a huge pink towel, and he trailed, bare-footed, across the corridor to his room. She closed the windows, to anticipate his habit of standing naked for the breezes to dry him. An orange moon was coming up over the cordia trees that lined the lawn. As yet it afforded only a little light. Soon it would grow less opaque, less red, and the dew on the grass would shine like fish scales. Christopher sat in his pyjamas on the window-sill to watch the moon. He knew that as soon as he was in bed Gip would draw the curtains and hide it. He no longer protested at this. His father said that Gip did it to prevent the queer shadows thrown in the room by the moonlight, shadows that might keep him awake. Christopher knew she did it because, like all negroes, she was afraid of the crooked-faced moon-woman. They believed that her light brought agues, and twisted the sleeping faces it fell on. Mr. Stevens said this was nonsense. " The devil give

men a little wisdom to make a bigger catch," was Gip's
rejoinder—and to Christopher this sounded impressive
and conclusive, though he wasn't sure what it meant.

Cinder had lighted the oil lamp before she went
home. Gip bent under its poor beam, continuing the
often-read story of Joseph. This and the Book of
Esther were her favourites and had therefore become
Christopher's.

The corners of the room were peopled with crouching
shadows. Christopher saw, and pretended not to see
them. All was well as long as Gip was there. But now
she had reached Jacob's setting-out for Egypt. It had
been a long day and her eyelids were drooping.

" Bed now," she told him.

Christopher said his prayers and slid under the thin
blanket. He tucked the mosquito-net under the side
and pulled it loose from the bottom of the mattress, so
that Boodles would not tear it when she climbed up.
After the curtains had been drawn Gip rocked and
dozed in her chair. She stayed until Christopher seemed
to be asleep.

Christopher was quiet only because he was thinking.
Try as he might he could not help suspecting that he
had been chiefly at fault in the day's activities. But
he had been punished for it, severely; and his mother
had not sympathised. He had not yet punished her
enough.

He heard Gip blow out the light and creep away.
He said nothing because his thoughts now were drowsy.
They seemed vaguely to be connected with the pattern
on the curtain. Moonlight shone through the cloth, and
following its dark trailings of stem, leaf, and flower was

like following a tortuous path, where underbrush tangled his footsteps and large grasping tendrils reached out to enfold him. In a minute he would have been asleep.

On moonlit nights the labourers in the plantation villages collected to sing hymns. Their hymns were Christian, but the rhythms to which they sang them were African, simple and repetitive, gaining speed and volume as they gained in length. In the churches the negroes had built for themselves, where untrained negro priests presided, the congregations beat time with tambourines. At night, in the open air, drums synco-pated.

Christopher's body grew taut as he heard the drums begin. The large and wandering shapes of half-sleep leapt upright and fused with the shadows in his room. He turned his face to the wall and drew the blanket up over his head. He listened—and knew he must not listen. The top of his head and his ears felt unnaturally sensitive, as if a hand was poised over them or as if someone was watching him. He was afraid to look. He screwed his eyelids more tightly against the fold of his cheeks and lay still. Perhaps if " they " thought he was asleep they would go away. Where he rested on it his left temple pounded, slowly and noisily.

The drums beat swifter and more loudly. He felt his body grow tight and small as their rhythm grew. If only he could call out! But he must not. Sweat bathed him as he contemplated the horror of betraying his awakeness. And if he did scream, his mother would come. Yet his fright, he sensed, was somehow connected with her. She must not come—not because his father would call him a baby, but because he did not want her now. She should have come before.

In the sudden silence between hymns he grew limp and cold. The shadows fell away from his bed and stood in shapeless waiting; then gathered again as he tensed once more with the drums. At some point, if he were not still as death, they would close right in upon him, and at their touch he would shrivel into nothingness. But if he could relax . . .

Mrs. Stevens sat reading in the drawing-room. She had not turned the pages for some time. In fact she had read the same paragraph over and over, ever since the drums had begun. She stared at her lap, glanced quickly up at her husband, and turned again to meaningless words. Christopher would call out if he was awake and nervous. She was sure he would call out.

It was much later that Christopher called out. The drums and the house had been silent for three or four hours, and he asleep much longer. But there had seemed to be no interval.

He was still listening to the drums; and around his bed waited the teeming shadows. Now they drew nearer, now receded, till the moment came that he seemed to have been expecting and dreading, when they lay beside and upon him, cold and dark in their weight and nearness. There was a sound of horses' hoofs beating evenly, and a pounding motion under his left ear, as if he lay on a jolting cart. The air clung heavily about his nostrils so that it was hard to breathe. Then something pricked his foot sharply. He screamed;

but the cry was muffled in the blanket that, in his sleep, he had dragged up over his face, leaving his body exposed to the wind. Frantically he tore it off and screamed again. This time Mrs. Stevens heard him. She came running, holding her nightgown bunched up in front to prevent herself from tripping as she ran. Her husband followed with a flashlight.

Christopher was sitting up in bed. In spite of the curtains moonlight flooded the room. He pointed at his foot.

" It bit me, it bit me," he sobbed hysterically.

Mrs. Stevens pulled the mosquito-net off the top of the bed and put her arms around Christopher. He hid his face on her breast.

" What bit you, Chris, dear? " she asked softly. " There's nothing there—only Boodles."

" Not Boodles," he whispered. " The lizard. The shiny lizard."

" There's no lizard there, pet. Look, Daddy will shine the torch. See, there's no lizard there."

He took his face timidly away from her caress. Boodles was licking her fur at the bottom of the bed, more concerned with the dew on her coat than with the light and intrusion. Christopher looked carefully around the room.

" There," he yelled, hiding his face again. " There's a man there! "

Mr. Stevens pointed the flashlight into a corner.

" That's your shirt on a chair."

But Christopher began to whimper again. " The drums," he said; " they were coming after me—and I couldn't scream," he said.

His father grunted. This was a familiar story, with a familiar ending. He gave in, gruffly.

" All right," he said; " come and get into our bed."

Christopher searched for his little pillow to take with him. He slept the rest of the night between his parents. He lay close to his mother and did not look up, because staring over the bottom rail of the bed were black faces with wide eyes and mouths that grinned. Their grins seemed to be telling him, " We'll get you another time."

3

Morning brought a clear hot Sunday. The sun slid horizontally into the room and made rainbows in Christopher's eyelashes. He was half-awake. Blackbird colonies just outside the windows were noisily conversing from tree to tree.

Christopher knew it was Sunday because his parents were still asleep. In some strange way they could always tell. During the week his father would have been dressed by this time. Christopher did not like Sunday as a rule. He preferred those days that he thought of as the even ones—Monday, Wednesday and Saturday. Sunday meant church, clothes that he had to be careful with, nothing to do, and silence in the plantation yard. It was a whispering kind of day.

He lay still for a minute. It seemed an hour. He decided to go back to his own room. Very carefully he crawled out, over his mother's legs. Her eyes flickered open and shut again. He stole away, carrying his little pillow.

But he did not go back to bed. He sat on the window-sill with his legs hanging down outside. There was dew all over the lawns. They lay like silver pages waiting to be written on. He swung himself gently down, until he felt his feet touch the storm-shutter on the basement window. After that it was easy going. He jumped backwards on to the flower-bed, leaving two deep foot-prints. These he hid by digging over the soil with his fingers. He walked around the long garden with its scented bushes of alamanda and ginger-lily, and then, starting at the left corner of the first lawn, began to make a pattern by dragging his feet across the wet grass. He made a diagonal, looked back to see its dark line waving unevenly through the dew, and crossed the driveway. The other lawn was a tennis court, regular in shape and therefore more satisfying to draw on.

Tiring of this he sat in the swing. He couldn't climb back to his room through the window, so would have to wait until somebody opened the back door. His feet were wet and cold. He decided to collect cordia seeds. They were cream-coloured and had a pleasant smell, but looked untidy on the grass. His father was always encouraging him to collect cordia seeds. But it wasn't a very interesting occupation. He wandered around to the back of the house. Cinder was just letting herself in by the kitchen door.

" Morning, Master Chris," she greeted him. " What you doing outside in pyjamas? "

" Everybody's asleep," he explained. " Can I help light the fire? "

Cinder didn't say no, so he trailed behind her as she unlocked the windows. Daylight streamed in, and cockroaches fled to their nests behind the cupboards and under the sink. She then opened the stove and shook the ashes out. Christopher brought newspapers and faggots. Piling them in, she threw on paraffin and applied a match. The burst of flames was succeeded by smoke.

" Faggots wet," Cinder grumbled. Vigorously she manipulated the damper and blew into the front of the furnace. Eventually the smoke trailed away. Christopher sucked an orange. He was rather a mess by the time Gip arrived. There was orange-juice on his chin; his pyjamas were wet, and muddy in places; he smelt of smoke. She scolded him.

" I had a bad dream," he told her. " I slept in Mummy's bed."

" Oh, dear! " Gip raised her eyes to heaven, then looked at Cinder for sympathy. " What you been dreaming now? "

Christopher decided that he'd better not tell. Nightmares did not frighten him in the morning; and he didn't want not to be told about the cholera again.

" Witches and grubs and things," he volunteered in an off-hand fashion—they being his pet aversions. Perhaps, though, he'd better be a little more specific. " I was swallowed by a—a—cow," he added.

Gip looked doubtful.

" A cow can't swallow nothing big as you."

" It was a big cow," he persisted; " big as the one they sawed the horns off." The remainder came in a rush. " But Clark killed it on Saturday, and when he cut it open I jumped out. Everyone was surprised."

Gip asked no more. She would not encourage him in his fancies. She did not believe he had dreamt about cows at all. And Master Chris was altogether too fanciful. For her little distinction lay between imagining and lying. Both condemned their perpetrators to eternity of hell-fire—somewhere inside the earth, where Satan kept his kingdom, as the negro pastor had taught her. They never said anything much about hell in the parish church where she took Christopher at eleven o'clock; but the Sunday-night sessions at her own chapel had made her very aware of its existence.

This was not the Sunday for church however. Once a month the family had breakfast with a sister of Mr. Stevens who lived by the sea—a huge breakfast at eleven o'clock, consisting of black puddings, souse, and other kinds of offal from the pigs that had been killed on the preceding Saturdays. Christopher was not interested in the breakfast. But he loved the sea, and felt in kinship with its infinite moods and inhabitants. He knew this was one of those special Sundays because Gip took a brightly coloured shirt out of his drawer instead of a white one. He would wear sandals and no socks, and could be perfunctory about washing because he would wash in the sea later. He barely restrained himself from jumping up and down. It seemed such a long time since he had last been to the sea.

" Don't forget my bathing-suit," he ordered, " and a box to put shells in."

Gip laughed. This was the nearest she ever saw to excitement on Christopher's face. Little boys, she thought, should be excited most of the time, not solemn and using long words like a grown-up. But then, with only grown-ups around, how could he be anything else? She wanted to hug him; but Christopher was impatient of affection at this point.

" Hurry up," he said, as she fumbled with a button.

" Lord, Master Chris, there's no hurry. The master and mistress ain't even had their tea yet."

" Yes," he insisted, " but I have things to do before I go."

" What things? "

" My sn. . . ."

And then he remembered! He wasn't to have snails any more. A horrible thought struck him.

" Gip, you don't suppose Daddy won't let me go? "

" Why should he? "

" Because of yesterday," he reminded her. " The snails."

" Heavens, your father's forgotten that now," Gip assured him.

But Christopher was not so easily convinced. Excitement left him. He finished dressing, silently and methodically.

Nor had his father forgotten. When Christopher came out to the car, Mr. Stevens looked sternly at him.

" You shouldn't be allowed to go to-day," he said; " after yesterday's performance."

Christopher felt himself on the verge of tears. He had feared this, and, almost automatically, he turned to go back into the house. Gip was standing at the bottom of the steps. She held him.

" You don't mean that, Master Stevens," she said. It was a statement, not a question.

Christopher thought that the wind had suddenly died, although he had noticed no wind. He watched his father. Behind the group Mrs. Stevens sat in the car. She was frantically motioning to Gip to go away. The old negress stood her ground. Realising, perhaps, what was coming, she pressed Christopher against her. Ralph Stevens blanched. His hands were trembling.

" How dare you? " he spluttered at last.

Christopher had seen his father in a rage before. There was nothing he feared more, even when he himself was not the object of anger. It made him feel as if his stomach, grown red-hot, was slipping out between his legs. He broke away from Gip and ran into the house.

He did not hear what was being said. He did not want to hear. And when, a little later, Mrs. Stevens came to fetch him, she found him hiding in a wall closet, crouched among the hanging clothes, dry-eyed and shivering.

" Come, Chris," she said gently, taking his hand; " we are just going."

He went obediently, his face pale and expressionless —though when he saw his father waiting in the car, with silence like a cold space around him, his hand grew taut, as if he wanted to pull away from her.

" Where's Gip? " he whispered.

Mrs. Stevens had already decided on her lie. " She isn't going to-day. She wants to go to church."

Christopher looked at his mother suspiciously; but she did not return his look. After all, she argued, this would not be the first time he had gone without Gip.

But Christopher's suspicions had been merely instinctive. He could not, in fact, conceive of a world without Gip. She was as much a part of his life as school and holidays, food and play. She had always been there, always would be. It never occurred to him that his father might have dismissed her.

The route to his aunt's house was familiar and un-exciting. They passed a few people, walking or in donkey-carts. Christopher inspected them all carefully, deciding by their clothes whether they were on their way to church or to the sea. He felt a little superior to those who looked like church-goers. In each plantation village a laughing group was collected around the public water-pipe. Some of the group waved at the car as it went by. He did not wave back, knowing that they waved at the car, not at its occupants. Hens rushed from under the wheels.

Christopher had his breakfast before the grown-ups, who ate late and stayed long over it. Meantime he was despatched to the beach—with a whole series of injunctions on this particular day, since Gip was not there to take charge. He was not to go into the water until his parents arrived; he must remain in the shade; not eat too many sea grapes, nor climb coconut trees—no matter how horizontally they grew; and, generally, get up to no mischief. He wondered vaguely, as he set off through the avenue of casuarinas, exactly what he was supposed to do. Everything had been forbidden him—except gathering shells, which, anyhow, could hardly be done without venturing out of the shade.

For a time he collected dried almonds and pounded them. But the kernels were tiny, and he was far less expert than Gip at breaking them open. Invariably he hit his fingers with the stone used for cracking the shells, or squashed the soft flesh of the nut so that there was only sand and shell where he tried to extract pulp.

The distance from the house to the sea was about a quarter of a mile, through thick woods of casuarina and coconut palm. Christopher took a long time reaching the shore only because he knew that he "would get up to some mischief" once he arrived there. Normally he ran most of the way, leaving Gip far behind; but to-day, without Gip, he was trying to make the time available for mischief as short as possible; and, after he had lingered over the almond-pounding, he hunted sea grapes. It was the wrong time of year for them; but, as a gesture, he pulled a handful of hard green berries and idly threw them at crabs. The crabs in the woods were yellowish, like the sandy clay in which the casuarinas grew. They had black beady eyes poised prominently on stilts. He wondered how they managed to keep the sand out of their eyes when they dug their holes. A snail could always fold up its stilts when there was danger; but the crabs did not even have eyelids. They saw him coming, no matter what his direction, and scuttled away at completely unpredictable angles. They were really most stupid-looking.

At last he reached the shore. Remembering his instructions he stuck firmly to the shadow-line, looking for shells in the dead sand along the edge of the woods. But the sand there was old and dry. The sea had not washed it for years; and what shells might once have lain there had long ago been bleached and broken by the sun, so that they too had become sand. It was most uninteresting. He ventured nearer the water, still keeping within safe distance of the trees in case voices warned him of his parents' approach. He went slowly up the beach, bent double, searching the wet edge for puppies' eyes and auroras.

Time passed; and the sun climbed to its noonday height. There was now no wind. The aspen feathers of the cassuarinas continued to shiver and sough as the heat rose, like crooked panes of glass, from the sands. Christopher was being most successful in his search. Already the box was half-full. But he too was feeling the heat. Occasionally he ran down to the sea and cooled the soles of his feet. He splashed water over his neck, because Gip had said that this was where sun-stroke developed. His parents were taking a long time; but he no longer remembered them. Nor did he realise how far up the beach he had wandered. He was hardly aware of moving, because the shells came in clusters. He was now on his knees sifting the sand through his fingers. This was the only way to find green peas—a particularly small shell of a rich emerald colour. The negro fishermen sometimes made bracelets by stringing them on fine wire. Perhaps he could make a green and pink necklace by interspersing them with puppies' eyes.

The sand shifted under his eyes. He wiped the sweat away with the back of his hand, but his vision did not clear. He looked up. The waves of heat that he had noticed before, flowing over and rippling the shapes of things, seemed to have drawn nearer. They played in his eyes, so that when he looked at his hand it had a queer movement, as though he were waving it in front of a crooked mirror. He had better go and lie in the shade until he felt better. He stood up; violent nausea seized him. He thought he was falling. There were men coming down the beach towards him. He yelled at them to frighten them away. But they came on, red horsemen riding black horses; and under the horses' hoofs deep shadow spun in giddy circles. Then all grew black as they reached him and trampled him down. The shells spilled as he fell fainting. Later the tide would come in and wash them back into hiding, because the man who came up the beach, who saw him fall and carried him up to the house, had not thought of the little wooden box and its treasures. He had thrown out the remaining shells and used the box to fetch water for Christopher's head; and he had left it then, to float away with the other driftwood.

4

THEY WERE coming again, the horsemen; but now no longer leaping, scarlet like fire. He could see their silhouette reared dimly against the dark, hoofs poised, beyond and then upon him. He rolled over on his back out of their way, and sat up.

" Quick, Daddy," he yelled; " bring the gun."

It was quiet in his room; a moment ago he had thought himself cold; now he was hot and sweating. His head throbbed, and he wanted to be sick. Why didn't somebody come?

Mrs. Stevens came, bringing a lamp. She seemed relieved to see him sitting up in bed.

" I'm going to be sick," he whimpered.

She handed him a basin. While he bent over it she refilled the ice-bag and pressed it against his forehead. He was not sick. He felt as if he should be, but nothing happened. He explained.

" Lie back," she told him. " It's only when you move your head."

He lay back on the pillow, with the ice-pack on his forehead, still clutching the basin.

" Where's Gip? " he asked. " I want Gip."

" Daddy's gone to get her," Mrs. Stevens soothed him. " She'll be here soon."

That, at least, was true. It had taken her nearly an hour to persuade her husband that Gip must be brought back. They should soon come. Gip, fortunately, would not refuse to come.

She felt a trifle lost. The doctor had told her what to expect, what to do. But Gip did these things instinctively. She had always taken charge when Christopher was ill, ordering Mrs. Stevens around with an authority that no one thought presumptuous. Perhaps her remedies were obscure, superstitious even —the Jacob's Court leaves, herb tea, and liniments she so grandly called " embrocations "—but they seemed to work.

Christopher had again dropped off to sleep by the time Gip arrived. She sat on a chair beside him, rubbing his hands in a kind of therapeutic caress and mumbling prayers. She prayed on such occasions, a rambling old wife's talk, heavy with sighs. No one heard her. Christopher slept on. He had not known when she left: he did not know she had returned; and in the morning when he woke he took her presence for granted. But that was a symptom of his illness, because sometimes during the days that followed he moaned again for her, as he had on the first evening. This happened when his fever climbed dangerously, the sundown delirium. Then he seemed to be asleep, but his head turned from side to side as though searching a comfortable place on the pillow. At other times he slept genuinely; yet would waken and appear to know what had been going on around him while he slept. Then he was peevish about the oil and leaves Gip had plastered on his chest and stomach. They itched, he complained. They drew the fever out, she scolded him. Always he knew when it was time for his food and medicines—as a baby does, Gip explained to herself. But she did not profess to understand the workings of the human mind; in fact she had always been too reverent to allow herself thought on the matter—though now even Gip was startled out of her pious acceptance.

The third night had been a bad one. Christopher had mumbled most of the time. Once he had knelt in the middle of the bed and delivered what sounded like a sermon—except that it had been composed of noises instead of words. About three in the morning he had fallen quietly asleep, and Gip had gone to bed. She was up again, and dressed, when Mrs. Stevens came in at seven. Christopher was still sleeping.

" I think that must of been the bad time," Gip told her. " He'll be getting better now."

" He looks dreadful," Mrs. Stevens disagreed.

" Maybe. But he's not so tight. His jaw's no longer clenched nor his forehead creased. They's good signs."

" His hair needs cutting." She could think of nothing better to say, and said it to soften the contradiction she had implied previously. The straight dark hair, long around Christopher's face, did accentuate his illness, the pallor and prominent bones. She noticed, though, as Gip had said, that the mouth no longer worked, nor was the brow drawn tight over the eyes, as if to shadow some fierce brightness. Gip broke in on her thoughts.

" You going to send him to his grandparents' when he better? " she asked.

Mrs. Stevens felt herself stutter, mentally, at the

suddenness of the question; she knew that the old woman's eyes were watching her in amusement.

" I don't know," she said at last, looking down at her feet. " I hadn't thought of it."

" Well, it's about time you did then. The boy needs a change. He too nervous altogether."

Mrs. Stevens did not retreat. Instead she shot for sympathy.

" You know that his father doesn't want him to stay there," she said. " He hardly ever takes him to see them —and then only for the shortest time possible."

" Why? " Gip's tone was aggressive. She recognised the piteousness of her mistress's situation but chose to take advantage of it. She knew the answer to her question—or thought she knew—but wanted to hear it put into words.

" He says they spoil him. They have so much money and can do so many things for Christopher that we can't."

" A good thing too. He ought to be glad. The boy don't have much of a time. He ought to be glad to have family who can help."

Mrs. Stevens's lips grew thinner.

" They didn't help much when Ralph was in debt and Christopher on his way. And—God knows—we could have done with help then."

In spite of the bitterness in her voice Gip continued the attack. " They might have had reasons," she suggested soothingly. " There's always two sides to a question, you know."

" There was only one side to this," and now Mrs.

Stevens spoke loudly and angrily. " They didn't like Ralph because his family was better than theirs."

" So Master Chris reaps the bad feeling? " She spoke sadly, though with a certain satisfaction in being able to make the criticism. " No wonder he feels like he wasn't wanted sometimes. Children know these things." She turned to look fondly at him, as if the still figure in the bed could confirm her words. Instead Mrs. Stevens saw blankness fix on her face, as though the movement of her head had suddenly killed all sensation. She realised that Christopher's eyes were open. Automatically she stepped into the silence.

" Hallo, Chris! Been awake long? "

Christopher did not answer immediately. When he did, he turned his eyes in her direction, without moving his head.

" No," he said. " Can I get up this morning? I feel fine. And can I go and stay with Granddad Fraser when I get up? "

" I suppose so," Mrs. Stevens took the plunge. " He hasn't asked you yet, though."

" He's always 'asked me,", Christopher told her petulantly. " But you wouldn't let me go. He told me I could come any time I wanted."

" Well, we'll see; but I don't think you're better yet."

Christopher looked at Gip to see if this was true. She nodded her head.

" When I am better then," he concluded.

But Christopher had not exhausted the subject. Twice during the day, when he was alone with Gip, he reverted to it.

" Don't they really want me? " he asked the first time. His forehead was puckered with curiosity. There was no trace of tears. Had he been tearful Gip could have handled the situation more easily. Soothing him with endearments she could have avoided an answer and, at the same time, have laughed his self-pity away. She went on sweeping the room.

" Of course they do," she said. " I was just exaggerating because I wanted them to let you go to your grandpappy's."

She watched the effect of this out of the corner of her eye. Christopher was gazing straight ahead, his eyebrows still creased in thought. But he said no more at the time; and she made haste to talk of something else, to coax him out of his seriousness.

His second attack was more oblique. He was too young for logic, but out of the staccato disharmony of thought he produced the revealing question. Gip did not underestimate him. She knew that he had been thinking along these lines since last she had evaded the point.

" What does it mean," he asked, " when somebody's better than somebody else? "

" That depends," she stalled. " White people is better than black people—mostly. That's because we work for them. But all is one in heaven, black and white together."

" I know that," Christopher told her. " It's in one of my books. And yellow people too. But I mean white people. Are some white people better than others—when they don't work for them I mean? "

Gip hesitated. She had not thought about it.

" Maybe," she said at last, " if one lot of white people had been to school more, or . . ."

" But Daddy left school when he was fourteen to go and work. I heard him say so. Is he still better than Granddad? Didn't Granddad go to school? "

" Yes, but Mr. Stevens's family is old. They came from England long time ago, before the slaves was freed. They had a lot of land and money in England."

" Where did Granddad's family come from? "

" I don't know nothing 'bout your granddad's family, except that they was poor and Mr. Fraser made a lot of money heself."

" What happened to Daddy's money? We don't have any now, do we? "

" It went, bit by bit, I expect. And your daddy lost the last after the war, when all the planters went poor —and the merchants rich. That's how your granddad got his money. That was just about the time you was born, though, so you wouldn't remember. But your daddy used to spend money like water before them days."

Christopher subsided. He didn't understand this business of money. It seemed awfully important. His father had once had money, and now he didn't. He was certain about this second point, because every time he wanted something awfully badly he was told that his parents couldn't afford it. Granddad Fraser could always afford it; but he wasn't allowed to ask. His mother was as strict about this as his father. Yet Granddad Fraser was *her* father. Couldn't she get money from him? It was necessary that he understand this business of money. It had something to do with what Gip had said about his not being wanted. He would ask Grand-dad when they let him go to stay.

And what did they mean by saying that somebody was better than somebody else? To be good just meant not to be naughty, and all the people he loved were good. Gip, he was sure, was quite as good as anybody else. Because she worked for his father didn't make him better than she was. Besides, his father had been working for Grandfather Fraser when he was born—yet they had said that his father was better than Grandfather Fraser. It was all nonsense, and most mixed up. He felt weary with the effort of thought, and fell asleep again.

5

Gip HAD been right about Christopher's illness. After the third night he recovered rapidly; and somehow Mrs. Stevens managed to persuade her husband to let him spend a few days with her parents. Mr. Fraser came for him on the afternoon of the tenth day, by which time Christopher was walking around, still weak from the high fever and recurrent nausea, but lively and excited at the prospect of staying at Belfield. His visits there had been short, and had never taken him beyond the main living-rooms; but these had been enough to stimulate his imagination. He coached Cinder in her cat-feeding duties and Oslin in the watering of his plants. What qualms he might have had about leaving Boodles and the garden, to be underfed and over-watered, left him as soon as his grandfather arrived in the big shiny car he always hired. Christopher was most impatient with him for spending an hour discussing rainfall and sugar prices with his parents—dull topics that grown-ups seemed to enjoy. But he made up for his silence then by telling the chauffeur on the way into town all about the horsemen who had ridden him down; and by repeating the story to his grandmother and aunt later. It was a story that grew colourful in retrospect and by repetition—and Gip was not there to mar its brilliances by warnings of hell-fire.

Belfield proved quite as exciting to explore as Christopher had imagined. In the rambling upstairs were six bedrooms, large and tall, filled with huge furniture and dozens of paintings and photographs. Everywhere he went the strange eyes in the pictures followed him. But they did not terrify him like the portraits in the long corridor at home, that were dark even in daylight and at night collected the tossing shadows of oil lamps around their hands and faces, making their subjects point and stare. They were cosy people in the pictures at Belfield, fat and friendly. The rooms, too, were lit by electricity, and during the day sunshine flooded in, till the dead portraits seemed to smile, approving the vista of lawns and gardens they regarded from above.

To reach the lawns from upstairs one went down a wide circling staircase, through two heavily carpeted living-rooms, to a verandah flagged with grey and black tiles. Tall white columns supported the roof of the verandah, and leading down from it, almost as broad at bottom as the verandah itself, swept another flight of steps, smooth and grey. On the right of the asphalt yard in front of the house was a tall hedge. Through arches cut in the hedge one reached the rose gardens beyond. On the left were tennis courts, while the yard itself narrowed to a lane and disappeared winding down an avenue of canopying mahoganies. At the back of the house were fruit trees and a lily-pond with ducks. It seemed to Christopher, this first evening, that thousands of people should live in so large a space, that he would never have time to see and know it all. The arches in the hedge fascinated him particularly. They led into a world completely separate, where fairy-book creatures might live—though he could not expect to find them in so confusing a place, from which they could escape by one archway when he entered by another. The roses were an experience in themselves, all colours, wonderfully scented and named. His aunt told him their names, Gloire de Dijon and Julien Potin, Laurent Carl, Maréchal Niel—words he could not remember, musical like his mother's piano-playing. Roses, however, were too big for his triangle at home. Perhaps his aunt would give him cuttings from the carnations and snapdragons that grew under them. The carnations were clove-scented and deep crimson. They seemed to grow wild whilst the snapdragons gaped at him with open mouths that showed tinted throats and furred, yellow tongues. He had seen them before, but never in such a profusion of shades. He passed quickly by the zinnias and calendulas. They had no smell and looked stiff in spite of their brilliance. He didn't want any of them, and hoped his aunt wouldn't suggest it because he was a little afraid of her and thought he might have to accept the offer.

Christopher had always been afraid of his Aunt Margaret. He had not met her very often, since she never came to his father's house. She was large, unlike his mother but like the rest of her family. Her arms and legs, however, were thin, and deeply tanned from her work in the garden at the wrong time of day. Her most terrifying feature was a small mouth, pencil-lipped and red, like a knife wound on the sallow skin; and she had a habit of pursing her lips angrily, till even the red disappeared. She ruled the servants and her parents with sour words and violent threats. She was always promising to knock people's heads in, or to push her arm down their throats. Christopher had never seen her do either, but was impressed by the possibility since her eyes widened and sparkled fiercely as she made the threat. On the other hand, his grandparents never grew alarmed; sometimes he even saw them wipe faint smiles off their faces. He watched her tirades fascinated, open-eyed-and-mouthed. Once she caught him at it. He blushed and looked hurriedly away. But she said nothing to him, only tossed her head and sat back, simmering and seeming to enjoy the impression she had made on him.

Early in his visit to Belfield Christopher discovered that it was not his father that Aunt Margaret disliked, but his mother.

Possibly Christopher would have done no more than wonder at his aunt's seemingly perverted sense of affection, but for the fact that he had been told, more than once when he had asked his mother why Aunt Margaret never came to Surrey-house, that she and his father " didn't hit it off too well." This he had accepted: and now was proof to the contrary.

He and his aunt were walking in the rose garden one morning, when he came upon some snails' eggs under a clerodendron bush. She wanted him to smash them. She did not like snails, not even after he told her how they ate the blight off fruit trees. She asked how he knew about such things.

" I used to keep snails' eggs," he told her, recalling the pleasure wistfully.

" Don't you any more? " she asked.

" No," he said, kicking a pebble. " I went into the fernery to get them when I wasn't supposed to go into the fernery; so Daddy made me throw away all I had."

" That was probably very sensible of him. What did your mother say about it? "

" Oh, she would have let me keep them."

" She's foolish enough to let you keep anything," Aunt Margaret observed crossly. Christopher thought she said this only because she did not like snails; but, anyhow, he didn't like his mother being called foolish.

" She's not foolish," he declared hotly. " She's just as clever as . . . as . . . you."

He hadn't meant to be rude, and now he was a little frightened. But Aunt Margaret only smiled.

" Maybe," she said thoughtfully after a moment. " Maybe." And they continued walking.

Later he tried to apologise. " I'm sorry," he said, " about just now. But Mummy is the "—he paused to find the most impressive adjective—" the bestest person in the world—except maybe Gip." He pondered a moment, then added, " I think, though, I like them about equal."

" Better than your father? " Aunt Margaret asked.

" Oh yes." Christopher did not hesitate.

She stopped and turned to face him.

" You should love them equally," she told him.

" Should I? But Daddy's always so cross. He makes me cry sometimes. Anyhow, he doesn't like me, so why should I like him? "

54

" Because he's your father. And who says he doesn't like you? Of course he does."

" Why did he take away my snails' eggs then? And he nearly didn't let me go to Aunt Jessica's that day I got sick. Of course," he thought it out for a minute, " if all that hadn't happened, I wouldn't be here now."

" Do you like being here? "

" Oh yes," he said enthusiastically. " It's very large; and there's such a lot to do; and Granddad and Grannie are the nicest people . . ."

And then Aunt Margaret did a strange thing. She bent over and kissed him. Christopher blushed. But she had already turned away and was continuing her stroll.

" Your father's a very fine man," she said. " He may be cross sometimes, but then he has a lot of worries."

" About money, you mean? "

" About money." She sighed. " And your mother doesn't help very much."

" You mean she should get some from Granddad and give it to him? " Christopher grew eager. It seemed as though he had at last found an ally in his line of argument. But Aunt Margaret disappointed him immediately.

" No, I don't," she said. " Your father wouldn't take it anyhow. I mean she shouldn't spend so much herself."

" But she doesn't," Christopher protested. " I've often heard her say she never has any money to spare."

" Certainly she doesn't." She spoke almost to herself. " But if she asked for the moon Ralph would have a darn good try at getting it for her." Then she added, by way of explanation, " If your father worried himself less, trying to make her happy, he'd have less inclination to be cross with you."

She said that like a preacher, Christopher thought to himself, and grew silent, sensing from her tone that the discussion was at an end. But he went over it all later, when he was sitting alone by the lily-pond watching the ducks.

She doesn't like Mummy, really, he decided—a duck stood on its head in the water and wriggled its tail to reach farther down—but she likes Daddy. I wonder why they always said it the other way round—he threw a pebble at a drake that was bearing down on the duck; the drake flapped across to the other side of the pond and waddled out—I don't believe she'd bash anybody's head in—another duck, a muscova this time, came swimming out from the reeds, followed by five yellow fluff-balls—she couldn't know Mummy very well or she'd have to like her—he stood up and reached out to pull a pink water-lily—I like her though; not as much as Gip, of course, and Gip likes Mummy better than Daddy, and Gip is bound to be righter—he had to pull the lily with all his strength; and that, for the moment, occupied him. When the stalk did come loose from the pond bottom he fell suddenly back on the bank. A long brown stem came with the flower, slimy in texture and smell. He pounded it between two rocks to enable him to break it shorter. I must remember to ask Granddad about the money, he told himself, as he carried the flower in to his aunt.

Those days were all sunny, and the nights without terrifying shapes. By nature Christopher would have tended to think of light and darkness as the negroes did —as the opening and shutting of an eye; but his upbringing had estranged his nature, so that, until now, he had regarded the sun rather as a lamp, lighted, like the oil lamps and storm lanterns at home, to bring respite from the shadows, the dreams and the fright. At Belfield he slept when it grew dark because he, like the sun, was tired. He woke, eager for the newest sights, the variety that the sun would reveal that day.

But he never did ask his grandfather about the money. An embarrassment had grown upon him since the intention first budded, like a blight sucking his innocence. There was no explanation for it. It dated back to the discarding of his snail collection, forced upon him as that had been and all the events resulting from it.

There was ample opportunity for questioning his grandfather. Together they went shopping on Saturday morning. Grannie Fraser saw them off in the car with an injunction to her husband that perhaps Christopher was not meant to understand.

" Now don't spoil the child," she said. " It'll only make him miserable when he goes home."

The chauffeur drove off. This, thought Christopher, is a good time to ask.

" Granddad," he ventured, " are you really awfully rich? "

His grandfather laughed. " Not awfully," he said. " I have enough though, to be comfortable on."

" Oh." Christopher sat back into the long deep seat; but his legs did not touch ground so he slid forward again. " Where are we going? " he asked.

" To buy a toy," he was told.

" Oh." He pondered in silence for a moment. " What kind of a toy? "

" You don't seem very keen," his grandfather observed teasingly. " Don't you like toys? "

" I don't think so." Christopher knitted his brows. " I haven't had very many,—and I didn't really like those very much."

" Good heavens! Never heard of a boy who didn't like toys! What would you like then? Tell me all the things you would like and I'll choose one for you."

Christopher considered the suggestion seriously.

" Well," he drawled at last, " I'd like a paint-box like Mummy's, to paint pictures with, and brushes and knives and things. A new fork for my garden, and some snapdragon seeds like the ones Aunt Margaret has; a big china dog; and, yes, some new books. All mine are torn and the pages keep falling out. They must be fairy stories, though, like Grimm and ' The Heroes,' or else about boys at boarding school." He thought for a moment. " And that's about all, I think."

" Not a very big order," his grandfather remarked. " I was afraid you'd be asking for a bicycle or an electric train or a gun or some such thing. Wouldn't you prefer a bicycle or an electric train to any of those things? "

" Well, perhaps instead of the fork. I can really make my old one last longer; but not instead of anything else."

" What a strange little boy you are." Mr. Fraser looked at him keenly.

His affection made Christopher shy. " Oh! " he said

for the third time, looking away and out of the window.

" Wouldn't you like a real live dog instead of a china one? " his grandfather suggested.

" No, thank you; I don't think so. Daddy already has two dogs you know; and I have Boodles. Daddy says Boodles is awfully spoilt—and she wouldn't mind me having a china dog—white with brown spots and long ears, like the one Aunt Jessica had that got lost for six days and they found at the bottom of a well, still alive."

It was Grandfather's turn to be nonplussed. " Oh," he echoed, and lapsed into silence.

Christopher received all the things he had listed— except the snapdragon seeds. The shop they went to only sold packages with a single colour of seed. His grandfather would have bought several packages to obtain the variety Christopher wanted, but Christopher explained that he had only two empty beds and that there would be a waste. He seemed so definite on the point that Mr. Fraser did not press alternatives.

" Now we'll have a drink," he told him, when all the purchases had been made; " and then, home."

They had their drinks, Christopher an ice-cream soda and Mr. Fraser a rum punch, sitting on the verandah of Maynards, overlooking the main street. " People," Christopher thought as he watched the patterns of moving brightness, " are not interesting, like things. I would much rather watch the ducks in the lilies at Belfield—or a ladybird in my garden at home." Neither the sounds they made nor the colours they borrowed were as attractive as the sound of trees or the colours of plants. For the most part they were clumsy and loud-mouthed; and he was too young to recognise their invisible blossomings. The only flower of a being that he understood that day was, unfortunately enough, already overblown and hideous with canker.

When they returned to the car Mr. Fraser remembered another purchase he must make. Christopher chose to remain in the car inspecting his china dog. The chauffeur was smoking a cigarette on the sidewalk, chatting with the fruit vendors who lined the gutters with their trays. A shadow appeared the the window on Christopher's side of the car. He looked up, and drew away, pushing himself into the soft upholstery. But the beggar had seen him. He peered in, his face gaunt and hideous with sores.

" Beg for a penny."

" Haven't got a penny," Christopher managed to whisper.

" Yes, you have, young sir," the beggar wheedled. He pointed a trembling finger. " Look in your pocket there."

Christopher turned both his trousers' pockets inside out. He did not want to have to speak again. But the beggar was not satisfied.

" You old Fraser's grandchild, ain't you? You must have a penny for a poor beggar."

Christopher slid to the other side of the car and pretended to be studying the shop windows. The negro spat on the street. His voice rose, no longer whining.

" No need to be so grand with me, because I'm black," he said. " Your grandpappy got children black just like me."

Christopher began to feel dirty. His skin crawled, as

if he was being infected by the beggar's scrofula. The face pushed farther into the car, confidential now.

"Sure you got a penny, sonny. Be a sport. I ain't had nothing since morning gone."

Christopher tried to be firm with his quaking voice. "I told you I didn't have any money. I . . . I've spent it all."

The head withdrew with a shrill guffaw. "Heh! That's rich," it said. "Spent it all, he says." The voice approached again, menacing. "Spent it all didja? Well, do you know where you got it all to spend?— From bastards like me, slaving from first of January to last of December for you friggers . . ."

Christopher saw his grandfather coming down the pavement to the car. The beggar saw him too. "Little shit," he spat in an undertone before turning to transfer his attentions, cringing again. Mr. Fraser, who had not seen Christopher's face, automatically pulled a couple of coppers out of his pocket and handed them over, without looking at the man. The beggar gave Christopher a final leering glance, mingled of amusement and triumph, and shuffled off down the street. Mr. Fraser did not even notice the absence of the usual "God bless you." He climbed into the car and settled himself.

"Well," he said, turning to Christopher. "Good heavens! What's the matter with you?"

"That man," Christopher confessed shamefacedly. "He frightened me."

Mr. Fraser turned to look after the beggar; but he had already disappeared.

"Why?" he asked. "Did you know him?"

"No. But he knew me. He looked horrible—as if

he had—leprosy. And he said horrible things about me
—and you."

"Did he, by George? I'll get a policeman after him
—disturbing children and frightening them." He took
up his stick and made to get out of the car. Christopher
stopped him.

"Don't do that," he exclaimed, more frightened than
ever—and then, quietly, "Don't do that. He's gone
anyway."

"As you like." Mr. Fraser shrugged his shoulders.
"But we can't have that kind of thing, you know.
Begging from the people he's just cursed," he added in
an outraged undertone. He sat back again and the
chauffeur drove off.

On the way home Mr. Fraser tried to draw Christopher away from the subject; but Christopher answered
in monosyllables, brooding, it must be, on something
the beggar had said.

For Christopher the day grew suddenly oppressive.
He had known these moods before, when a single
incident affected everything else with its disturbing
qualities. Things that had passed without comment, or
even with favourable comment, showed their obverse
faces, and became unreal or irritating. Immediately his
purchases seemed unimportant—the china dog rather
silly, the paint-box useless, the books brief pastimes.
Even Belfield became a vexing interruption, there being
no permanence in its pleasure, there being no per-
manent pleasure. He did not know what was wrong
with him, why his grandfather should suddenly tire
him, why he should want not to be pestered by
questions and yet not want to be by himself. He knew

he was being unreasonable, but the necessity for being unreasonable was something outside himself, stronger than himself. He was glad when they reached Belfield; and in the business of displaying his gifts the mood lifted a little. Perhaps the fact that his grandfather was not present had something to do with it. Without him it became possible to forget the emotion even if he could not forget the event that had inspired it. In any case, it was not so much the beggar's face that continued to concern him as the beggar's words; but he was afraid to ask. One could not talk about such things—certainly one did not talk about white gentlemen having black babies. Once when a favourite cook had told him that she was leaving her work at Surrey-house to have a baby, he had said, " But you aren't married, are you ? " On being told she wasn't, he had stated triumphantly, " Well, you can't have a baby then. Only married people can have babies." The woman had hidden her face in her apron and run off laughing; but his mother had scolded him for mentioning such things. His innocence was not so great now—Boodles had had a litter of kittens, and cats didn't get married, but he still could not grasp the possibility of Grandfather having black babies. In any case there was no one he dared ask, so he might as well forget about it. Probably the beggar was foolish as well as dirty and ugly.

Another unpleasant thought came to the fore in Christopher's brain, helping to drive out the other. To-day was Saturday. Tomorrow evening his parents would come to take him back to Surrey-house.

6

CHRISTOPHER HAD never known this feeling before. It was more than a feeling. It hurt physically, as if something too big to be continued in him was pushing against the broad bone of his chest. Whatever he did, it stayed there. It had begun on Sunday, early in the day—so much so that he had hung around his grand-parents and aunt all morning and afternoon, as if fearing that to be away from them would increase his pain. For the same reason he had wept when telling them good-bye, and sobbed softly to himself all the way home in the car, because, as he had dreaded, the ache grew unendurable. He had gone to bed exhausted, too miserable to notice even Boodles.

When he woke in the morning the sun was just rising. The sky looked sad in its hushed dawn-colours. He searched for the familiar things in his room at Belfield. But this was not Belfield. It was a silent, lonely place, grey outside, with sighing birds and curtains that flapped with a melancholy slowness. He buried his face in the pillow and endured this new and strange misery.

A little later he climbed out of bed and washed. There was still no sound of anyone stirring. Now I will clean my teeth, now I will hang up my pyjamas, now

64

I will put on my shirt, my pants, my shoes, now I will comb my hair—he made a list of things as he did them, trying to busy his thoughts with ordinary and usual functions—anything to keep from thinking of Belfield; and, as he repeated the name in his mind, a sob caught at his throat. Quickly he turned to something else inconsequential. I'll go down to the orchard all by myself swing in the Chili-plum tree Gip won't catch me still cool in the orchard so early before the birds start to sing sun to rise lizards in the orchards won't be awake perhaps they never sleep why have yellow tongues under their throats instead of in their mouths can't think of anything else to think about quickly enough will have to stop. . . . He ran down the corridor down the back stairs into the kitchen hardly noticing the scamper of cockroaches, opened the yard door—and out into the clean damp morning air. The earth smelt good with the musty sweetness of after-rains.

In the orchard bottom a sinuous mist had gathered, so that the thick black trunks of the mango trees and the mottled grey-fawn of the guavas came, rootless and stunted, out of white earth. Christopher ran into the mist as into hiding, but it swirled away from him as he passed, seeming unwilling to touch his body and cloak his misery—or like the problems of recent weeks, that foamed out of his reach as he grasped at them. He climbed the plum tree and sat with a branch between his legs, head and back resting vertically on the trunk. Underneath him the mist folded back, thin where he looked down, opaque and complete beyond.

The mist intrigued him. As soon as the sun's rays slid over the orchard wall it would evanesce, and lie in mercury drops on the banana leaves, or sparkle in the spiders' webs. The trees would regain their colours and contours, and the film of concealment disappear in a silver pleasure of dew. But the pain returned, condensing to sorrow in his eyes. For a long time he sat motionless, hardly thinking. Then, as the sun climbed and the mists went, his thoughts fused to a final determination. He must know why his father disliked him.

Gip came for him. She knew where to look when the back door was open so early—on the lawn, in the triangle, or swinging, forbiddenly, on the Chili-plum tree. Christopher saw her toil down the steps on the far side, almost level with his perch. He swung down, raced up to her and flung himself in her arms. She saw the tears shining on his cheeks before he wiped them off on her apron as she hugged him.

" Why, Master Chris," she held him at arm's length, " you've been crying."

He turned his face away from her. He was afraid he'd cry again. " I didn't want to come home," he said.

" Not want to come home! " Gip pretended to be astonished—and then hurt. " Not to see Boodles and me? Cinder looking after Boodles so well, and Oslin watering your garden? "

" Has he? " Christopher laughed feebly. " And nothing dead? "

" No, nothing! " Gip spoke in the drawling singsong reserved for special confidences, as though Christopher's attempt at conversation had been seriously inquisitive. " In fact, they all look better than ever."

She took him in and gave him his orange-juice and toast. " What you going to do now? " she asked.

"Don't know," he said, gazing dispassionately out of the window.

"Well," she jollied him, " I have to tidy your room. Why don't you come and look at those new books while I do it? They certainly is beautiful books . . ." she went on, leading the way down the corridor and talking as she went to keep him with her, body and mind. It had been her doing, she told herself as she settled him on the window-sill with his new possessions and turned to make the bed. She had persuaded Mrs. Stevens to send him to Belfield, and now she must help him back to his former life. It had not been an unhappy one; but would he remember that now?

Gip sighed as she straightened up. Her rheumatism was always bad these damp mornings.

Christopher was playing with his paint-box, opening each tube of paint and smearing the uncapped head on a sheet of paper. Miss May, his art teacher at the three-pupil preparatory school, would be thrilled with it. So far they had only drawn and crayoned. But school did not begin again for at least a month. Meantime he would paint Miss May some pictures of Surrey-house. But what was the use? He couldn't paint anyhow. He put the paint-box aside.

The day passed in a Sunday fashion—existed rather than lived. Gip kept Christopher by her most of the time, encouraging him to paint, to dig, to read—all of which he performed obediently but without enthusiasm. The plantation yard was alive with its usual Monday activities, but Christopher shut himself in a world that its sparrow chatter could not penetrate. Everything seemed to lead him back to Belfield. Once Gip, trying to stir up his old keenness, had asked, " What you going to plant in them two empty beds you got there? " At the time he was lethargically cutting the dead flowers off a pentas.

" Was going to plant snapdragons in them. Aunt Margaret gave me some. But I forgot them."

On another occasion they had strolled down to the pond. Gip pointed out a white gaulding sitting on the bough of the calabash tree, the newest mongoose holes —but all Christopher said was, " They've got pink water-lilies in the pond at Belfield—and a mother duck with five young ones."

Eventually even Gip tired of his unresponsiveness.

" Master Chris," she addressed him seriously, " you must wake up. You can't live remembering the good things passed. That way is a sure waster of time. You always enjoyed yourself here." She began to plead with him as, self-consciously, he pulled a grass and sucked its soft stem. " Why can't you do the things you used to like doing before? You got your garden, your books, your animals—and this is your home, where you got to live. You'll have to make the best of it and forget Belfield—in that way at any rate . . ."

Christopher's eyes flooded again. " You don't understand," he sobbed. " It's not Belfield."

Turning, he ran away from her, paying no attention when she called after him.

Leave him be, she thought. Maybe he'll get over it faster by himself. But she closed her eyes momentarily and whispered a prayer.

And Christopher was glad to be by himself. Gip's

presence all day had been like a cloud over the sun, prolonging dawn and the mists. He had not wished to hurt her feelings; but with her near him, watching him, not with her eyes but with her mind—as he could sense —he had been unable to grapple with his problems. He had chased wildly among them, and made such confusion that he had seen no more than the athleticism of their escapes.

But now he ran after them. They kept a little ahead, unswerving, and tiring when he tired. He heard the patter of their footsteps growing louder with the pounding of his heart; and when he fell exhausted at the foot of the Chili-plum tree, they were already there, waiting for him in the dry leaves.

Christopher turned over on his back and stared up at the sky. The sun was setting and its light dribbled through the chinks in the green canopy and splashed in sudden melting coins around him.

Money, he knew; it was something to do with money —his grandfather's money.

But when he thought of money and his grandfather, and then tried to see his father's face without his knowing that he was looking at him, he saw instead the beggar in Nelson Street.

He shook himself and sat up. But immediately he saw it again—his father looking at him with the beggar's eyes. And this time he did not flinch from the look. He stared back with a calm curiosity. He did not even question it. It had come to him naturally—just as the shadows and the drums had together conjured up the black nightmare figures; just as the noon heat and loneliness had mounted a sunstroke and clothed horses and men in red and giddy darkness. He saw his father spitting at him as the beggar had spat—because there was no one else to do it to.

Christopher came in to dinner late, untidy and un-washed. A dead leaf clung to the seat of his trousers. Sliding into his chair he took up the soup-spoon mechanically, as if still dreaming. His father called him. He did not hear. Mrs. Stevens nudged him. He looked up, startled.

" Yes? " he said.

" You haven't washed, or combed your hair, Christopher."

" Oh," Christopher answered unemotionally. " I forgot."

" Well ? " Mr. Stevens's voice began to rise. " Aren't you going to go and do it then? "

" Yes, sir." Christopher went off down the corridor. When he returned his father was expounding angrily. " If it affects him this way," he was saying, " he won't be allowed to go again, that's all there is to it." He turned to Christopher. " And you'd better listen too. If going to Belfield so overwhelms you that you can't remember your manners, then you won't be able to go again."

Christopher stared at his father. His face was expres-sionless, but his eyes intense. Mr. Stevens looked away. He continued, grumbling to himself, " If it had been left to me you wouldn't have gone in the first place."

Christopher was not expected to answer this. He did; and his insolence was cold with a strange new authority. His father had looked away from him, had said less than he had intended to; and Christopher's stare had been an unconscious challenge. He had not known it at the time, had not done it on purpose; but now he knew, and was glad he had done it.

"Yes, sir," he said gravely. "I know."

Mr. Stevens started to his feet. "You impertinent little puppy," he thundered. "Go to your room and stay there till I come."

Christopher went. He went calmly, no longer afraid of his father's anger. Nor was he afraid of the caning he knew was coming. Self-possessed and proud he sat waiting on the window-sill. He felt as if he had won a victory; and even if defeat strengthened his father's hand, he had still won. Never had he been farther from tears.

And when it was all over and Gip came, as usual, bringing solace, she found him busied with his paint-box, painting a picture of Surrey-house for Miss May, the art teacher. She knew at once, by his dry eyes and the self-conscious way in which he pretended she was not there—she knew that Christopher was no longer a little boy—and knew it sadly, because it meant that from now on he would rely on her less and less; and though her prayer had been answered—in a kind of fashion—she was not yet ready to treat him as anything more than a little boy.

"But there will be others," she thought, "to help him along. There is always others."

Part Two : The Mother

7

OVER ONE EYE Old Rose wore a patch that had once been black and was now green. She carried a bag under her apron of the same ancient material.

Christopher was afraid of Old Rose. He always hoped his mother would be near the back steps when she arrived. If she wasn't, then *he* had to deliver the weekly sixpence. Sometimes, if Rose was still down below talking to Essie or Cinder through the kitchen window, he could lean over the rail and she would hold out her apron to catch the sixpence; but at other times she had already come up the steps before he found his mother and returned with the money. Then he had to put it into her hand, and Rose's hands were hardly less terrifying than her eye-patch. The fingers were long, and knobbly with rheumatism. They curved inwards, ready to pounce. Christopher never ventured his own fingers too close. He dropped the sixpence in and hurriedly retreated. From between the jalousie slats he would watch until she had gone. Perhaps she didn't notice that he never waited to receive her blessing; she spoke it to the end nevertheless. Or perhaps she knew that he stayed behind the door. Not much escaped her one bright eye; though she carried a stick, she never hesitated going down the steps, never seemed to use the stick except to tap news of her arrival.

One day the strings that held Old Rose's bag broke. A shower of cents, pennies and sixpences rolled down the steps. Forgetting that she wasn't supposed to know he was behind the door, Christopher ran out to help. As he picked up the coins he handed them to her, one by one.

" That's all," he said at last.

" No, Master Christopher. One missing, one of the white ones."

He found it under the scraper at the bottom of the steps.

" Here it is." He held up the sixpence triumphantly.

This time he wasn't quick enough. As Old Rose's hand closed on his, horror quivered through him. He tried to pull away, but the fingers held him tightly, convulsively. Only when she had bent and pecked at the back of his hand did she release him.

He would have fled then, except that Rose stood between him and the back door and his knees were made of water. In his ears the blessing she uttered mingled confusedly with the sound of his own heart beating. Afterwards the only thing he could remember was the way she had crossed herself. He remembered that and he remembered the cook's insistence that he go and wash his hands immediately. Of course he would wash his hands; but he didn't see why she should be so frightened. Old Rose hadn't grabbed *her*. But she was new because Essie, their own cook, was ill, and he hadn't talked much to her yet. He wished, though, that Essie would get better and come back. He didn't like going into the kitchen with a strange woman there.

" She did it so," he showed Cinder, imitating Rose's final gesture.

" The old hypocrite," was all Cinder said.

But Gip knew. She had been to a Roman Catholic church, and she recognised the sign of the cross even from Christopher's unorthodox thumbing.

" Then she made a cross," he told his mother later, " on her stomach, like this, and then she went away. I was frightened, but not as frightened as the new cook. I don't think I like the new cook," he added in brackets. " But I won't be frightened any more. She mustn't kiss my hand, though."

" There's no reason to be frightened of an old woman," his mother said.

" She only has one eye."

" Well, so does that woman you told me about who brings Miss Bea's bread."

" Addie? Yes, but Addie's eye is just closed up—as if it was asleep."

" Old Rose's eye looks just the same underneath the patch."

" Yes," he said as he moved away, " but I don't see it underneath."

The next time Rose came she had a new eye-patch. It was again black, but somehow less terrifying. Even so, Christopher was glad his mother was present. It gave him sufficient courage to ask if she had put fresh strings on her bag.

" It wasn't the strings," Old Rose told him, lifting her apron. " It was that rotten old bag. Miss Beale give me some cloth an' I get a new one make."

The new bag was the same colour as the new patch. Christopher appreciated the importance of their matching.

" Like Mummy," he explained to Gip; " when she wears a white hat she always has a white bag too."

" I wonder why she doesn't have a red patch," he added as he trailed off, ". . . or a pale blue one."

Christopher was always trailing off in the middle of sentences. Everyone noticed, and Ralph Stevens had commented on it.

" What did you say, Christopher? "

But Christopher had looked blankly at him.

" Why, nothing, sir."

He hadn't said anything. He had merely gone away leaving his thoughts suspended in sound behind him.

But Gip suspected that Ralph Stevens might not always let the matter pass so easily.

" Master Chris," she called him back. " Don't you know that only mad people talk to themselves. You goin' end up in Jenkins."

" Have you ever been in Jenkins? " Christopher inquired. " Tell me about it."

Gip laughed. It was an old trick.

" You're a sly one," she said. " But the last time I tell you 'bout Jenkins," she added severely, " that night you screamed the place down. I ain't goin' tell you again."

" Do you think the new cook knows anything about Jenkins? " Christopher asked.

But he was already on his way to find out.

The new cook looked astonished when Christopher

suddenly appeared in the kitchen and, without pre-
liminaries, posed his question.

" You know? " he continued impatiently. " Jenkins.
Where the mad people go."

But perhaps she didn't know.

" They keep them behind bars," he explained; " and
they put their heads out and scream and bite. Gip says
you go mad if a mad person bites you. It's called rabies.
But Mummy says that's only dogs."

The woman's jaw dropped lower. Obviously she
knew nothing. Christopher tried another tack.

" Do you think Old Rose is mad? " he asked. " Was
that why you were frightened and made me wash my
hands? But she didn't bite me, you know. She only
kissed it, there, on the back. She has whiskers like
Aunt Blanche. . . ."

The woman turned away.

" You best not have nothing to do with Old Rose,"
she muttered. " She bad."

" Why? " Christopher wanted to know. But he
didn't hear her reply. " Why is she bad? " he persisted.

He had to ask a third time before she would tell him.

" You ain't never heard of obeah? " she inquired
irritably, and left before he could think of another
question.

Outside in the sunshine, among the splendours of his
triangular garden, Christopher momentarily forgot Old
Rose. There was a more interesting problem on hand,
in the form of a huge cassia that grew in the hen yard
but whose roots pushed into the garden and sucked the
goodness away from his, more delicate, shrubs. He had

frequently hinted to his mother that it would be a good idea to cut down the cassia. It had flowers, yes, but only once a year, and they soon became long pods full of smelly black gum. The pods were brittle when they fell and, smashing open, sowed young cassias in all directions. The seedlings looked like dahlias and he had frequently been fooled. But Mrs. Stevens had either been unsuccessful in making her husband appreciate this point of view or else she had not tried.

Christopher hacked at the roots he had uncovered.

" Maybe Rose could put obeah on it and kill it," he told himself.

He didn't know what obeah was exactly, except that people who practised it were able to do all manner of strange things. The word seemed, however, to be in the air. Apart from what the cook had said about Rose, he had heard Gip and Cinder use the word a couple of days previously. They had stopped talking as soon as he came up. He had been angry. Nowadays they were always whispering together. When he asked what they were whispering about, they either laughed or told him that he was too young to understand.

Suddenly bad-tempered, Christopher jabbed his trowel into the mat of roots and left it. He would go and look for humming birds in the orchard. Maybe all the ripe guavas hadn't been picked for stewing.

But meantime, whilst he worked, the sun had become overcast and the air grown tense and still. It made him want to hit things and, at the same time, too hot for the effort that that would require. The breezes that now and then touched the leaves into petulant gossip seemed to circulate only in the tree tops. The orchard lay in a hollow of land, and it was even stiller there. The green drooped listlessly. He climbed a mango that grew straight and tall and peered over the other trees. Eventually there was only sky above him, but a sky whose greyness sat on his shoulders and wouldn't be pushed away. He wondered if snails felt the same way about the shells that held them down.

Perhaps there was going to be a storm. At this time of year there were always supposed to be storms. The fishermen stayed ashore, and at table they had sea-eggs instead of fish. He hated sea-eggs—as much because the sea-egg divers threw the shells into the surf and you stepped on them and got prickles in your feet when you went swimming, as because of their strong briny taste.

For all that, he had never seen a storm. It might be a pleasant change. The last time there had been a hurricane, Gip told him, the sea had washed right into Fairmont churchyard. The church had collapsed and all the records that were kept there had been destroyed —so that afterwards nobody knew who was married or who his parents were. The tombstones had been over-turned, coffins smashed, and the skeletons inside thrown around. For months afterwards people kept finding skulls and bones on the beaches.

It had all been very horrid but, he was sure, very exciting. In any case, they were safe at Surrey-house. St. Paul's was the nearest church and that was miles away. Anyhow, the sea couldn't get that far. Even a tidal wave couldn't get that high or that far. But, for the moment, it was amusing to imagine that the stretch of green below was the sea, that he was safe in his tree-top house, and that he could at any time climb down and cool himself, holding on to the mango tree and paddling in the water below.

He dangled his feet down and splashed among the leaves. But it was rather dull sport and eventually he climbed down altogether. On the sea-floor Gip awaited him.

" Master Christopher. How many times I got to tell you not to climb so high? Suppose you fall? What I goin' tell the mistress when I take you in in pieces? "

" Do you think there's going to be a storm, Gip ? Will St. Paul's churchyard be washed away? "

" Certainly not. Whatever put that notion in your head? "

" Well, perhaps a *little* storm then? And if I cut some more roots maybe the wind will blow the cassia over— it must blow from that side, of course, otherwise it will fall the wrong way—and then I won't have to ask Rose to put obeah on it."

" You don't put obeah on trees, Master Chris. You put it on people."

" Can Rose do that? " Christopher asked incredulously. " And what happens to them? "

" It all depends. Sometimes they . . ." But she caught sight of the expression on Christopher's face, and stopped.

" Come along," she said, " it goin' to rain."

8

THERE WAS no storm that day, nor the next. It merely rained, heavy black rain that hid the valley and broke the flower-heads with the weight of its falling. Ralph Stevens was confined to the house and Christopher, so as not to annoy him, almost entirely to his bedroom. By turns he painted and read and talked to Gip; but it was all rather boring. He wished school would begin again. . . . Not that that would help, of course, because, in such weather, he wouldn't anyhow be able to go to school. Even if the buggy did not leak, it would be impossible to keep the rain from blowing in. And then he caught a chill and developed tonsilitis. The wetting and the tonsilitis were unpleasant, but the horse's behaviour on the slippery roads was what he feared most of all. Normally the most tractable of mares, Popsy had a habit on rainy days of putting her four feet together and sliding down Carrington Hill. Sometimes the manœuvre was successful; sometimes the harness broke and Popsy fell on her haunches. Once she had smashed the buggy against the hill face. Being nearer school than home, they had limped on to school. Donald had left him there and taken the buggy into town to have the wheel repaired. Not knowing what had happened, Miss Bea had grown angry when he couldn't say his tables. He couldn't because there were butterflies in his stomach and he thought he was going to be sick. Finally he burst into tears.

" Popsy slipped and the buggy hit the wall . . ."

He tried to stop the tears, but they wouldn't stop; and Miss Bea petted him, which made it even harder.

He was too old to cry now but, if the same thing happened again, he wasn't sure he would be able to prevent himself.

Instead of thinking about such an embarrassing event Christopher decided to pay the new cook a visit.

She was busy. It was nearly dinner-time and she answered his questions in monosyllables as she moved from kitchen to pantry sink and back again. On one occasion Boodles ran between her legs.

" Get outa my way, cat."

She swung her foot angrily. She missed, but the attempt was sufficient. Christopher went white with rage. He snatched up Boodles.

" Don't you dare kick my cat," he shouted at her.

The woman put down the saucepan and faced him, arms akimbo.

" If it's your cat, you keep it outa my kitchen. Kitchens ain't no place for cats."

" It isn't your kitchen," Christopher shouted back. " You only work here. And Boodles can go where she likes. It's just as much her kitchen as yours."

The cook laughed grimly.

" Why you don't let it cook the dinner then? You done turn the animal stupid already." She turned back to the sink, muttering. " Treating a cat as if it was

84

human." She blazed back at him, " The food you give that foolish Boodles you would better give some half-starved child in the tenantry."

" That's none of your business, you—you . . ."

" And don't you call me none of your high-falutin' names, young man, or I'll tell your pappy 'bout you. And now you get outa my way too—and take that cat with you. I got to get the dinner."

" You wait," Christopher told her. " I'll . . . I'll . . ." His imagination stumbled. " I'll tell Rose about you," he concluded at last. " She'll put obeah on you, you wait and see if she doesn't."

The woman almost dropped the saucepan. But Christopher did not wait to see the effect of his words. They had been much lamer than he would have liked.

" Master Christopher," she called sharply.

But Christopher was halfway up the stairs and, though he looked back briefly, he did not stop.

He went and sat on the window-sill in his room and watched the rain. In the flower-bed under the window the ginger-lilies were lying flat in the mud and the salvias looked as if Boodles had methodically sat on each in turn.

Mrs. Stevens came in a few minutes later.

" What was all that shouting downstairs, Christo-pher? Like Millie Gilkes at the standpipe. You'd better be glad your father didn't hear you."

" The new cook tried to kick Boodles," Christopher protested hotly. " That's all."

And he returned to staring out of the window, arrogantly, as though the matter was, as far as he was concerned, over and done with.

85

" If your manners were no better with her than they are at the moment," his mother told him coldly, " then I should think that *you* were in the wrong."

Christopher kept his profile towards her. His right cheek burned as if she had slapped him and tingled as though waiting to be slapped. But she had never done it before, and now, after a moment's hesitation, she turned on her heel and left him. Out of the corner of his eye he watched her go. He did not move; but he saw nothing of what he was looking at—the rain descending in thick lines and the lawn a square grey puddle. He stayed where he was until Cinder rang the dinner bell.

9

Next morning the sun shone as though it had not, for the past two days, been playing truant. Light peered inquisitively into every cranny of the rain's making, and some, at least, of the flowers raised their heads to gaze back in interest.

Much to Christopher's surprise Gip laid out his beach clothes on the bed.

" But it's not Sunday," he pointed out.

" No, but you goin' all the same."

" Why? We never go except on Sunday."

" Don't ask so many questions, young man. Just be glad you is going." And a few minutes later she added, " And don't you ask no questions when your father is about. You know what he say? "

" 'Little children should be like old men's beards ...'" Christopher mocked solemnly. " But that doesn't mean me any more because I'm not little and I'm not a child."

" What you is then ? " Gip laughed. " A grown man, I suppose? "

" Well, not little, at any rate," Christopher pouted.

She did not tell him, but it was Gip's opinion that since Christopher had moved out of the " baby " class at school, and into Miss Bea's form with other boys of his own age, he had, in fact, begun to behave much less like a grown-up and more as a child should. He still had a fondness for wandering off on his own, with a vacant stare in his eyes. He was still, on occasions, uncomfortably solemn; and his rages broke as violently—but that he couldn't help; he had come by them honestly. Fortunately, though, they didn't seem to clash now with Ralph Stevens's. He had learnt to say nothing in front of his father; in fact, he seldom mentioned his father. It was as if, for Christopher, the older man had ceased to exist, to exist, at any rate, as a force moulding his life.

For Christopher, the only disappointment about this unexpected visit to the sea was the fact that he was not being allowed to swim. None of the grown-ups was going in, because, after two days of heavy rain, the sea would be cold and muddy, and probably rough into the bargain. A small stream ran along the edge of his uncle's property—through the ill-fated graveyard of Fairmont church. After a downpour it ran full, red-brown with the riches of eroded soil and all the summer's gathering of leaves. Foul at the best of times, its trickles normally disappeared into the sand before they could taint the surf. But now, along all that shoreline, the waters would heave, sickly opaque, heavy with churned mud.

Christopher's disappointment waned when he reached the beach. In spite of the sunshine the sea looked cold and unfriendly. Instead of the waves advancing in line against the shore, they scattered without pattern. Along the fringe of wet sand they had deposited a froth of dark brown moss.

There were always shells clinging to sea moss. But before Christopher set about exploring his find, Gip insisted that they go and look at " the river."

" If this was still a churchyard," was Christopher's only comment, " there would be lots of bodies floating on it now."

" You got a horrible mind, Master Christopher. You'd spend your time much better looking for shells. But leave your sandals on," she called after him. " There's sea-eggs about."

He wore his sandals, but they were soon squelching wet. It wasn't possible to keep one's nose in a nest of moss and one's eyes on the wash of the tide. From the point of view of green peas and puppies' eyes the hunt was not very successful. But halfway down the beach he found a fish. Its scales still shone, arguing that it was not long dead. And when he poked a stick into the gills and lifted them, they showed red underneath.

Holding the fish by the tail, he rushed back up the beach to where Gip was in conversation with a fisherman. The man had an old sugar-bag half-heartedly wrapped around him, but he carried neither net nor sea-egg pole. He seemed to be swearing as Christopher approached.

". . . so all we can do is wait," he said.

Gip noticed Christopher waiting on the fringe.

" What you found, Master Chris? Lord! " She threw up her hands. " A stinking dead fish. Throw it away, sir, and go wash your hands."

Christopher appealed to the fisherman.

" It's not stinking, is it? Look." He held up the fish

so that Gip could see better. " It's still silver. We can eat it."

" You don't eat dead fish—least, not them that's died naturalways," the fisherman told him. " Would be all right for bait, though—supposing that any boats were putting out."

" Oh well," Christopher shrugged, and threw the fish on the sand. " Aren't you catching anything to-day? " he asked.

" Water too muddy," the fisherman said tersely. " Can't see nothing."

" When it isn't muddy," Christopher wanted to know, " what does it look like—underneath, I mean? "

" Why . . ." The man scratched his head. " Why, it's like Fairmont parish church," he smiled, winking at Gip.

" But Fairmont parish church is all tumbledown," Christopher told him indignantly. " It doesn't even have a roof on or . . . or anything."

" That's what I mean," the fisherman said. " It's like Fairmont parish church—even to the weeds growing where the pews was. Weeds like those . . ." He pointed at the mounds of brown moss on the beach.

" I thought it would be all blue," Christopher said hopefully.

" Oh, it's blue all right, but mostly black . . . except where the sun shines."

" Perhaps it's like Fairmont parish church when it had coloured windows? " Christopher suggested.

" Um-m. . . . Maybe." But he wasn't convinced. " If Fairmont parish church had fish swimming around."

" After the last storm did you find any bones when you went sea-egging? The time the church got blown down, I mean, and all the coffins smashed open? "

Gip laughed. " At that time, Master Christopher, he was a little boy no bigger than what you is now." She turned to the fisherman for confirmation. " Maybe he wasn't even born yet."

But the conversation was taking a line Christopher didn't care for. He thought he would get it back into more interesting channels.

" Can you put obeah on people? " he asked. " I want somebody to put obeah on our cook. Gip can't," he added disparagingly.

" Don't know nothing 'bout obeah," the man muttered.

" Oh well," Christopher sighed. " Old Rose will have to do it. Do you suppose," he said, pretending a sudden earnestness, " that Old Rose could turn her into a . . ." —he looked around for something horrible into which Old Rose could metamorphose the cook—" into a fish? " He pointed at the mullet he had discarded. " A dead fish? "

" What nonsense you does talk, Master Christopher," Gip interrupted crossly. " You read too many fairy-tales. You should read your Bible stories instead."

But the fisherman only laughed.

On the way back to Surrey-house Christopher informed his mother that he had decided to be a fisherman when he grew up. At home he tied pebbles in the corners of his handkerchief and spent the afternoon searching for moths and butterflies to capture in his

" net." Any that he caught he promptly released. It was only the throwing that interested him.

That night, too, he was a fisherman. He dreamt that he went diving for sea-eggs in the reefs beyond Calais point. Underwater it was not at all what he had expected. There were stone pews for the fish to sit in, and an organ playing. The pews, though, were empty, and Jerusalem Stars grew between them. Overhead was bright blue, and he could see the sun. It had silver streamers hanging from it that vibrated with the waves.

While he was looking at the sun, a fish came through one of the windows. It swam up to him. He thought it was a mullet but it turned out to be the new cook. He wondered if she would try to bite him. But just then there was a splash and she swam hurriedly away. This time it was the fisherman who entered. And now he had nothing on, not even his sugar-bag. Christopher wondered what his father would say—in church too.

10

In spite of a dubious reputation as a person, Francis Walcott was highly esteemed as a doctor. After Christopher's birth he had warned his sister-in-law against having another child. Now, eight years later, she was pregnant.

This was the reason for the mid-week visit to Fairmont that had so surprised Christopher. There had, in fact, been several previous visits, but since he had been at school most of the time it had not been difficult to keep the knowledge from him. The visits were by now no more than routine. Eight years was a long time and, so far as could be seen, the pregnancy was advancing satisfactorily. It had been arranged, however, that should anything unusual happen—and, in any case, when the moment came in a couple of months' time— Mary Stevens would stay at Fairmont so as to be near a doctor. She had done the same when Christopher was born. Meanwhile there was opportunity for getting Christopher accustomed to the idea that, sometime in the near future, he would be left alone at Surrey-house with his father. She did not mention the matter to Ralph, knowing beforehand what his reaction would be; but for her it remained a problem.

The first attempt at preparing Christopher was not a success.

" Christopher," she began, " you wouldn't mind being here at Surrey-house with only Daddy, would you? And Gip, of course, and . . ."

" Yes, I would," Christopher pouted. " Where will you be? "

" Well, suppose I had to go away for a short time. You wouldn't mind my going away for a short time? "

" Yes, I would," Christopher repeated more emphatically. " Why can't I go too? Suppose I get frightened at night and you aren't there? "

" But you're a big boy now, Christopher," she wheedled. " You don't have bad dreams any more."

" Yes, I do," he frowned; " and if you aren't there, then I will."

At her sigh of resignation he brightened.

" But it's all ' suppose ' anyhow, 'cos you're not really going away."

The discussion was postponed for the moment and Christopher went off to his fishing. He had already invented a more complex sport. Out of an old piece of mosquito netting he had fashioned something that more nearly resembled a fishing net. Its middle was tied to a length of cord and its edges weighted with pebbles. Apeing the swing of the body and the flight of the hand that he had seen fishermen using, he cast his net out over the duckpond. The result was an occasional thousand or a tadpole. The tadpoles he preserved in a jar for his own amusement. The thousands he threw back so that they might continue their work of eating mosquito larvæ. He was hoping that he might capture some other creature in his net, some strange animal that no one knew existed in the pond. If one called the pond a " mere," there was infinite possibility: Grendel had lived in a mere, and Beowulf had gone there to kill him. There was no telling what lived under the lily-pads in the centre of the pond. Something obviously did, because when his father had anchored a raft there and built a pen on it to save the nesting ducks from mongoose, the ducks had been slaughtered and the eggs sucked just the same as on land. Christopher didn't understand why, when ducks swim so well, they had just let themselves be eaten—even if they couldn't have saved their eggs. At any rate, it had proved that Boodles wasn't the culprit, because Boodles hated water and couldn't swim.

No one had actually accused Boodles; but before Boodles's arrival Christopher had owned a dog. Even as a puppy Prosper had shown a taste for duck eggs. One day he had disappeared, and Christopher had been told that he had gone away for a few days to the dog doctor. In fact Prosper had never come back.

When, bored at last with fishing, Christopher returned to the house, he had four tadpoles and smelt of stagnant water. He found Old Rose waiting at the bottom of the back steps. It seemed less than a week since she had last been.

" Good morning, Master Christopher," she greeted him. " What you got there? "

" Tadpoles," he told her, peering intently into the jar. " I caught them with this."

" That's a very fine net."

" I know," Christopher said. " I made it. But there's

only tadpoles and thousands in our pond," he added, slipping past her and up the back steps.

As he went up the steps he saw the new cook move away from the kitchen window. He turned back.

" Don't go," he cautioned Rose. " I will find Mummy and come back."

" Rose," he said, when he returned with the sixpence. " Do you know about obeah? "

" Obeah? " she repeated. " Why I should know 'bout obeah? "

" Oh, I just wondered," Christopher said. " The new cook says you do though," he added challengingly.

" The new cook? What the new cook know 'bout me to shoot her mouth off for? "

" Well, it doesn't matter," Christopher soothed her. " I just thought you might because I'm looking for somebody to put obeah on her for me."

Rose wasn't soothed. She took the sixpence un-graciously and went away without so much as a thank-you.

Christopher was disappointed. He had been depend-ing on Old Rose and now it seemed as if, after all, she didn't know anything about obeah. For a moment he contemplated doing it himself. But all he knew was that people sometimes died if they found a bottle with a feather in it outside their doorstep; and though he planned on having his revenge on the new cook—more now as the result of a habit of thought than because he felt any great animosity towards her—he didn't plan on her dying. It would be enough if she had a night-mare and dreamt that Boodles swallowed her.

Life was suddenly empty and depressing. He had

exhausted the possibilities of fishing, and now he would have to give up his obeah project as well. Of course, there still remained the garden and the tadpoles—the tadpoles first. He'd have to put them where Gip wouldn't find them. She would never let him keep them in his bedroom if she knew.

11

Nothing took place at Surrey-house—in house, servants' quarters or tenantry—that Gip did not know of. She did not pursue knowledge: she attracted it; and for Donald, her nephew, she was a magnet. As groom he was both of the household and outside it. A mild creature, he had been known to weep when Christopher once fell out of the buggy between the wheels—an action for which Christopher rather despised him, on that occasion fright having dried up his own tear ducts. This same mildness made people speak in front of Donald as though he wasn't present. Hence his informativeness.

It was from Donald that Gip first learnt of the new cook's visit to the obeah-woman in Pegwell Bog.

" Where you hear it from? " she asked.

" Oh, here and there," he answered.

She did not pursue the point, appreciating that where obeah was concerned it was best to name no names; and she practised the same caution when she in due course relayed the information and Mrs. Stevens posed a similar question.

" What do you think should be done? " Mrs. Stevens asked.

Gip again evaded a direct answer.

" The servants won't like it," she said.

" But they don't believe in obeah, surely? "

" They won't like it nonethesame," Gip repeated.

" What Gip in fact means," Ralph Stevens interpreted when he in turn was informed, " is that they don't disbelieve either. Nobody knows, I suppose, whom she's trying to work obeah against? Probably some man—but it might be one of them."

" Or us," his wife suggested. " She may be trying to make sure we keep her even after Essie recovers."

" That's all nonsense, of course."

" Not if she starts putting things in the food, it isn't. And I don't think I want to wait till that happens. Shall I give her a week's pay and tell her not to come back in the morning? "

" You must do as you like, my dear. It might be better though, if you didn't encourage Gip to bring you these tales." More acidly he continued, " She seems able to put as fantastic notions in your head as in Christopher's."

" Would you prefer me not to do anything about it then? "

" You know perfectly well, my dear, that you have already decided what you're going to do. Or do you want me to do it? " he added petulantly.

" No, I don't think so." But she said it hesitantly. " What would the other servants think? "

" I don't give a God-damn what the servants think," Ralph Stevens's voice rose angrily. " Do you want me to do it or don't you? "

" No, thank you, Ralph," she soothed, firmly now.
" It isn't your job and, anyhow, I would prefer to do
it my own way."

Dinner that night was a dull, monosyllabic affair.
At sundown it had started to rain again, a slow per-
pendicular rain that would drip all night with the
precise monotony of a leaky tap. The sucks in some of
the field bottoms were already clogged, and Ralph
Stevens was contemplating the vista of half-drowned
canes that would greet him at dawn. His wife was
trying to eat naturally, but the thought that some
strange condiment might be in the food made each
mouthful more distasteful than the previous one. She
was wondering, too, how she could discharge the cook
without mentioning the word " obeah." Christopher
was merely bored. He had had an uneventful day,
when even imagination had failed him. Tadpoles didn't
become frogs quickly enough, and there was nothing to
do in the garden when the soil was sticky like putty. He
wished with all his might that something would happen.
But when he considered the possibilities logically he
could think of nothing that would, in fact, meet the
case. The most interesting prospect was to curl up in
bed and listen to the rain, with Gip nearby reading her
Bible or just rocking and dozing.

Cinder moved silently in the shadows.

" Like if the obeah working on them already," she
commented to herself—and saved up the remark to
share with her cronies later. Because her mind was
working in that groove she was the only one to show
any interest when, at the end of the meal, Mrs. Stevens
said:

" After the washing-up, Cinder, would you tell Cook that I want to see her."

She still didn't know what excuse she was going to give the woman for discharging her so abruptly, but, having taken the first step, a grey lethargy settled on her, and it was with a kind of panic that she roused later to the sound of Cinder's voice telling her that Cook was ready to lock up the downstairs.

So that Ralph would not hear what she said she chose to have the interview in the pantry. Cinder disappeared. Gip was with Christopher.

The woman was tearful when Mrs. Stevens told her that she would not require her in the morning.

" What I done wrong, mistress? " she asked.

" You haven't done anything wrong," Mrs. Stevens reassured her. " It's just that there is talk and—well, to save any unpleasantness it's best that you go now. As I told you when I employed you, it was only temporary anyway, until Essie recovered."

The woman looked up.

" What talk you mean, mum? I ain't heard no talk."

There was just sufficient challenge in her voice to enable Mrs. Stevens to cast her reply less apologetically.

" There has been, nevertheless. You probably know more about it than I do. In any case, I can't have the other servants upset. They've been here longer than you have, and if someone must go in order to keep the peace, then that one must be you."

" Who upsetting who, I'd like to know? " The woman planted her hands on her hips, and pushed her bosom out aggressively. " What lies they been telling 'bout me now? "

" I don't know whether they are lies or not," Mrs. Stevens told her calmly. " In any case I have made my decision. Here are a week's wages. I'd be glad if you'd take it and go quietly."

" Not till I've said what I have to say, I ain't goin'," the woman declared. " You white people think we ain't got no pride, that you can pick us up and push us back when and how it suit you. Well, it ain't always goin' be so." Her voice crescendoed to a shout. " You hear? It ain't always goin' be so. By that dead child you carrying I swear it ain't."

She turned imperiously; but immediately her anger broke. Throwing her apron over her head she rushed into the kitchen, sobbing loudly.

For a moment the other woman stayed where she was. When she could move, she put the money on the corner of the table and then, resting one hand against the wall, went back upstairs.

The fact that, next morning, Gip set about cleaning the upstairs of the house, while Cinder acted as cook, provided Christopher with a fund of questions.

" Where's the new cook? " he began.

" She's left," Gip told him shortly, hoping to forestall further enquiry.

" Then is Essie coming back? "

" No, not yet."

" Why did the cook leave before Essie came back? "

" You better ask the mistress that, Master Chris."

" Then she didn't leave! " Christopher exclaimed triumphantly. " Mummy sent her away. Why did she send her away? "

" Your mammie had her reasons," Gip informed him. " She didn't tell them to the servants."

" I bet she told *you* though," Christopher said over his shoulder as he left her to her sweeping.

" You better not disturb her," Gip called out after him. " She's resting."

Christopher came back.

" But it's only just morning-time," he protested. " Why is she resting now? Is she ill? "

" She didn't sleep so well last night," Gip said. " So you leave her be and go outside in the yard. I'll come when I finish."

" And don't climb no tall trees," she called after him as he disappeared a second time.

There was no incentive to climb trees. The mangoes were running wet after the night's rain and the guavas even more slippery than usual. Damp leaves touched him clammily as he passed and the spiders, busy repairing their webs, left loose threads hanging to smear and tickle his face. He looked disconsolately over the fence at the triangular garden. There was nothing to be done there either.

He trailed behind Best, the herdsman, who had just collected the cows' food. The various ingredients were kept in a long, locked bin and were measured out by the calabashful—so many of cottonseed meal, of linseed meal, oatmeal, pollard, coarse salt, molasses. These were then mixed together in a huge tub, with enough water to make a paste that could be moulded into large balls, larger than Christopher could hold. The cows came and took them out of Best's hands as he called each by name. Christopher sat on the top bar of the pen gate and watched them feed. They slavered as they ate, trailing cobwebs of saliva, and afterwards pushed their tongues up to their nostrils in a kind of face-washing. They came readily enough when called but, having eaten, were not so ready to give place to a new-comer. Occasionally there was a locking of horns, and once or twice Best had to enter the pen and whack an offender across the flanks.

Christopher was not exactly afraid of the cows, but he assisted only from the outside, with the aid of a long stick and loud yells of " Betsy," or whatever the cow's name was, " get over there." However, he had his favourites amongst them which, when their turn came, he protected from the others' greed with special ferocity. One cow in particular, called Diamond for the white star on her forehead, needed protection. She was a timid creature, due, Christopher maintained, to having been imported from St. Kitts. Imported cows were thrown overboard in the harbour and forced to swim almost a mile to shore. Diamond had never recovered from the experience. Unfortunately cows, unlike dogs and cats, did not understand one's attempts at being affectionate. Diamond backed furiously whenever Christopher tried to stroke her. His father maintained that Diamond was vicious in the plough, and he had had the top two inches of her horns sawn off—much to Christopher's horror. Best had assured him that the operation didn't hurt, but Christopher had refused the severed points of horn—although he had nothing like them in his collection—because he was convinced it must have hurt and that his father had been wrong to do it.

After watching the cows being fed, Christopher went to beard Cinder in the kitchen. But she was as evasive as Gip over the new cook's departure.

" Why is everybody so secret? " he demanded.

" Who is secret? " Cinder protested. " I ain't secret. I just don't know, that's all."

" I believe you're telling a fib," Christopher accused as he departed.

And he was sure of it when Cinder's laugh followed him, gurgling gleefully at his petulance. But he wasn't perturbed: his mother would tell him and then he could come back and tease Cinder with his knowledge —either that or she would have to confess to being a fibber.

" Gip and Cinder won't tell me why the new cook left," he complained when at last he found his mother. She was stretched out in a Berbice chair on the verandah, reading half-heartedly. She laughed.

" Why should they? There's nothing to tell."

" Of course there is," Christopher persisted, " because Essie hasn't come back and you said she would stay until then and if she hasn't stayed until then . . . then something happened. Did she steal something? " he inquired in a hushed tone.

" No, she didn't steal anything," she smiled. " She left because I told her to go and I told her to go because she was visiting the obeah-woman in Pegwell Bog tenantry." She drew breath at the end of the monotone with which she had been apeing him. " Satisfied now? "

Christopher looked astonished.

" But why did she visit the obeah-woman? And why did you send her away on account of that? "

" The servants didn't like it—and neither did I for that matter."

" Why? "

" Because she might have put something in the food."

" Oh," Christopher nodded knowingly. " You mean burnt hair and dung and things like that? "

" No I don't," Mrs. Stevens said indignantly. " Where on earth do you get such unpleasant ideas? "

" It was Gip told me that that was what they did when they want to work magic," Christopher protested.

" Well," Mrs. Stevens picked up her book again. " Let's forget about it. She hasn't put obeah on any of us, anyhow."

" Um-m," Christopher pondered. But his mother wasn't listening, so he kept his thoughts to himself.

He wished, though, that it were Rose's day for collecting the weekly sixpence.

When, a few days later, Cinder called from the kitchen door to tell him Old Rose had arrived, Christopher dropped his tools in the bed he was digging and rushed to greet her. By the time he got there he had forgotten exactly how he had planned on framing his questions. However, Rose gave him no opportunity.

" I see the new cook gone," she said. Then, as he did not reply, she added a complacent, " I glad."

Christopher's jaw dropped. He was suddenly afraid.

" I'll find Mummy," he mumbled, and dashed up the steps.

But as soon as he was in the safety of the corridor he

went more slowly. His thoughts raced as his footsteps dragged.

Mrs. Stevens was not in her bedroom, nor in the verandah. Christopher went out through the front door and circled the outside of the house. If she wasn't on the lawn and wasn't talking to Joe in the fernery, then he didn't know where she could be—unless she had come in from the other side and met Rose herself.

As he lingered outside the fernery door a high-pitched scream startled him. He turned to run in the direction it had come from. Cinder dashed out of the kitchen in front of him. She did not stop. She yelled at him over her shoulder.

" You don't come, Master Chris! You go back! "

But Christopher's legs moved under their own volition. His knees trembled as if they should give way, but somehow, and without his feeling it, his feet touched ground.

There was already a crowd gathered around the bottom of the back steps. He noticed Rose standing a little apart with hands clutched to her breast, panting. Then he broke through the circle. At that moment his father and Joe started up the stairs, carrying Mrs. Stevens between them. He only had time to see one side of her face, dreadfully pale and smeared with green; then arms grabbed him and Donald lifted him bodily away.

12

"SHE WILL be all right, she will be all right. Just a fall," Donald kept saying.

Christopher was not listening. It was over an hour since she had been carried indoors, and almost an hour since his father had rushed off in the car to telephone the doctor. His father had returned and the doctor had arrived soon after; but still nobody had come to call him or to tell him what was happening.

Hunched up, with his knees under his chin, and Donald's arm around his shoulders, he was waiting for Gip to come out and call him. She would tell him. She would tell him what was happening.

When Gip eventually appeared Christopher leapt off the bench and rushed at her, too quick for Donald to stop him. He threw himself upon her.

"Is she dead? She's not dead," he screamed; and the tears burst out.

Gip knelt down and gathered him against her.

"No, Master Chris," she said, pretending astonishment through her own tears. "She's not dead. Whatever put that silly notion in your head."

"Her face," Christopher choked. "It was all green."

"That was only moss," Gip soothed him, "where she scraped it on the wall when she fell."

" Can I go and see her? "

" No, Master Chris, not yet. The doctor's still with her."

" Can I then when Uncle Francis is gone? "

" Probably," Gip said. " But we can't stay here talking. Noise is bad for her. We must go somewhere where she can't hear us." She straightened up, but kept Christopher pressed beside her. " What you say if we two go and talk quietly in the orchard—where we can't disturb nobody? "

" Yes," Christopher said, with a catch in his voice. " Let's go and talk in the orchard."

Once in the orchard, however, there didn't seem to be anything to talk about. Gip answered distractedly, as though listening for some sound other than Christopher's voice. Eventually she must have heard whatever it was she had been listening for, because she then began to speak in an almost animated fashion.

" She was standing on the top step," she said, " talking to Rose. And then she leant forwards to hand her the money and, according to Rose, she seemed to totter as though she was giddy, and before she knew what happen the mistress had pitched she length down the steps. Luckily the master was there, and Joe, because they had been walking round the gardens, looking at it. And I was making the beds in the end room when I heard the commotion . . ."

" Somebody screamed," Christopher told her. " I heard it. Was it Mummy? "

" I don't rightly know, Master Chris. Maybe it was Rose."

" What happened to Rose? She didn't go inside too, did she? "

" No, she went in the kitchen to sit down for a while. She didn't feel so good neither after what she seen. She's getting on, you know. It gave her a real turn, it did."

It was Gip who, a short while later, suggested they should return. At first she was silent, but, as they neared the house, she once more began a nervous chatter. Christopher did not listen. He was only interested in seeing if his uncle's car was still in the yard.

It wasn't. And the yard was as deserted as if no one had ever been there.

" Everybody's gone," he interrupted. " Now can I go? "

" Let me go and ask Cinder first," Gip said.

But when they entered the pantry Cinder started to talk volubly and cheerfully, and Gip didn't ask her anything.

" Can I go now? " Christopher repeated stubbornly.

He did not miss the exchange of glances between the two women.

" Why are you looking at one another like that for? " he demanded. " Gip said I could go in when Uncle Francis left. Why can't I go now? "

" The truth is, Master Chris," Cinder began. " Well, it's this way, Master Chris. The doctor say your mammie need constant care and attention, so he took her with him in the car. She gone to stay with your Aunt Jessie till she better. Now don't . . ."

But Christopher gave her no time to finish.

" You knew," he whipped round on Gip. " You

knew all along. That's why you took me down to the orchard. You knew that I wasn't going to see her." He pounded his fists against her hip angrily, scarcely seeing what he was doing for the tears that filled his eyes. " I hate you," he cried. " I hate you."

And as Gip, careless of the blows, attempted to pull him to her, he snatched himself away and raced out of the kitchen.

" Oh Lordie," Gip sighed. " I might of known this would happen. And what now? "

" You better go after him," Cinder warned. " He ain't safe in that frame of mind."

" He won't do nothing. . . . Probably sit under that vine in the garden, or up the Chili-plum tree. He'll come back when the tears is over." She thought aloud. " But they didn't ought to take her away without him seeing her."

" What! " Cinder protested. " Lying there unconscious like a corpse, and her face all battered."

" It would still of been better. Master Christopher ain't so foolish as not to know a dead person from a living one."

" Well, he know better than me," Cinder declared, as she went back to the kitchen.

Muttering to herself Gip climbed the stairs. From the window on the landing she tried to peer through the canopy of thumbergia in Christopher's garden; but it was too far and its leaves too close. She went on down the corridor to Christopher's bedroom. Closing the door, she fetched her Bible off the shelf.

" Our Father," she began, as she knelt against the bed.

She did not open her eyes when, a few minutes later, she heard a rustle in the clothes closet behind her; and she did not alter the mumbling monotone of her prayers when, shortly afterwards, she sensed Christopher beside her.

Gip did not ask Ralph Stevens's permission, but that night she opened a cot in Christopher's room and slept there. The following night when he went to bed, Christopher looked around inquiringly.

" Where's the cot? " he asked.

And noting his expression, Gip quickly found an explanation.

" I have to wait till Cinder done in the kitchen. I can't move it by myself."

" Oh," Christopher said. But he lay sideways in bed, with his head propped in one hand, until the cot appeared.

He did not feel tired. He had done nothing all day to make him tired. Gip was snoring long before his waking thoughts patterned themselves into dreams.

If she gets better, he thought, giving shape to the prayers he had recited to Gip, I won't be bad any more, I won't be rude either, not even to Joe, though it's hard not to be rude to Joe, interfering old man; but still I won't be. It was Joe who helped Daddy take her up-stairs, and one arm hung down because he wasn't holding her properly. She only had one shoe too—I wonder what happened to the other; Rose must have picked it up because she was the only one there who could have. She looked awful, holding herself as if she had a pain and kind of yellow. She was frightened, I guess, she won't come back next week because there won't be anybody to give her sixpence, unless I ask Mummy for sixpence when I see her on Sunday. . . .

And on Sunday he went up the stairs to Aunt Jessica's spare room. But she wasn't there; so he went next door to Uncle Francis's bedroom, and then to all the other rooms. But she wasn't in any of them. Nobody was in any of them. He thought she might be hiding in a cupboard, because the rooms were full of cupboards—all the walls were cupboards. He wanted to call out; he couldn't though because the cupboards would all answer so as to muffle her voice, and they would echo his words one after the other and then all together, round and round the room, louder and louder. So he ran away with his hands over his ears. He ran outside, and through the woods for a long time before he was sure he wouldn't hear the cupboards and could take his hands away from his ears. He ran until he came to the stream at the edge of the woods—except that it wasn't a stream now, it was all part of the sea; and the tide was coming in fast. He asked the fisherman which way he should go, but the fisherman only laughed. So he ran back; but this time he had to run along the sand because the wind and the water had carried away the trees. And suddenly he was sure she was in one of the cupboards. She was in one of the cupboards, but only the sea knew which one; and because it knew it would get there before him, whilst he would have to open them all, one after the other, to find her. If only he could tell her that the sea was coming, that it had already washed away the trees and the churchyard. Then she would call out and he could go straight to her and let her out. He shouted as he ran, so that she would hear him coming and answer. But she didn't answer. There was a smile on her face because she was hiding from him and didn't know about the sea.

" Mummy, Mummy," he yelled.

Luckily Gip was there; somehow she must have known which cupboard it was because she had opened it.

" It's all right, Master Chris," Gip soothed him. " It's all right."

" She was in the cupboard," Christopher mumbled, " but you let her out."

And he was asleep again before he had turned his head over on the pillow.

On Saturday Gip took Christopher for a walk. They went down the hill towards the main road, the familiar direction of most walks but especially favoured on week-ends, when there was more traffic on the highway. From a crest of land beyond the quarry they could watch in peace, and comment—at least, Gip watched and commented: Christopher was frequently too far away to hear. He didn't really understand why it should be regarded as a treat to sit and stare at passing cars. There were other, more interesting walks; the cabbage palms at the end of the back drive frequently dropped huge sheets of bark, from which, with the help of a knife and drawing-pins, sandals could be made— not very comfortable sandals, but supremely original; or they could go through the tenantry where, at least, there were people—apart from the fact that a gully ran along one side, in whose dark bottom maidenhair ferns grew wild under wild breadfruit trees. But Gip didn't like the gully. Without specifying what she meant, she said it was evil, that anything could happen there. It was dark certainly, and twisty; but the most unexpected thing that could happen there was some strange-leaved succulent that Christopher had not yet added to his collection.

There was a sadness about this favourite walk of Gip's, something that had the quality of wakefulness in a world of somnambulists. Perhaps it was because at week-ends, when walks were usually indulged in, the plantation yard was empty and silent; no carts rattled along the road on wooden wheels, and the few villagers they passed were subdued out of recognition by shoes and formal attire. Perhaps it was because the people travelling in cars were distant and apart; one looked, and wondered where they were going, and it was friendly inside the car and cold outside.

But Gip liked it; and Christopher spent most of his time in the quarry. A path cut in the side wound down, and at bottom lay a bright white world, irregular where the limestone had thawed into caverns. It was always easy to see where blocks had been most recently hewn, since the quarry face was whitest there. Although there was nothing further to do in the quarry after he had inspected one or two caves, all of which were identical, it was more interesting to contemplate than the dusty road and the traffic that never slowed or stopped. Anyhow, Gip always summoned him when she thought he had been gone too long and was missing something of interest.

On the way home they met the new cook. Gip was panting slowly up the hill, too slowly to avoid stopping when the woman greeted them. She spoke affably.

" Good evening, Master Chris. How you is, Gip? "

" So-so," Gip told her. " The rheumatism comes and goes with the rains, you know."

" So they tell me. And how the mistress now? "

" All right, the last I heard," Gip said, almost creaking with the effort to move on again.

" I always knew that baby would born dead."

Gip glanced swiftly down at Christopher. He was staring at the other woman, with a heavy frown between his eyes.

" We better be getting on up the hill before the night dews catch us," Gip interposed hurriedly.

They parted. The woman went on down the hill.

Once or twice Christopher looked back. He waited till she was out of sight before he spoke.

" What did she mean about the dead baby? "

" She's a foolish nigger woman," Gip said violently. " She don't know what she talking about."

Christopher ignored the outburst.

" Is Mummy going to have a baby? " he asked.

" That foolish black woman," Gip grumbled. " What right she got to talk such things in front of a child." She turned to face Christopher. " Anyway, you shouldn't know about such things," she said severely. " Where you learn them from? "

Christopher looked astonished.

" What things? " he asked.

Gip swallowed and began again, hoping to cover up her mistake.

116

" Yes, your mammy goin' have a baby—at least, was goin' to before she had the fall. He ain't sure now, the doctor." She faced him again. " And don't you tell nobody I told you," she admonished, " least of all your pappy."

" But you didn't tell me," Christopher protested. " She did." He pointed down the road behind them.

" What happens to dead babies? " he asked a few minutes later.

" They bury them," Gip said quietly, " same as other people. But not in the churchyard, because they don't have no name."

" Where will they bury Mummy's baby? "

" Why you think they goin' bury it necessarily," Gip asked angrily. " You don't have to pay no attention to what that stupid Cook say."

Christopher asked no more questions. If Gip had been less absorbed in her own thoughts she might have noticed his withdrawal. She only noticed it later, when she was getting him ready for bed; and then, rather than stir up what might be dormant, she made no comment on the weary weight of his silence. Life had deserted him for the moment, and she could scarcely guess at what nightmares lay in ambush for the sleepless night-wanderers of his mind.

13

It was Thursday before Christopher saw his mother. On Sunday when he went to dress he found that Gip had laid out his week-day clothes.

" The mistress bad to-day," she told him, avoiding his eyes. " Maybe to-morrow you can go."

And somehow he lived through Sunday, with Gip to lift him over the hurdles of hours. But it was the same on Monday.

" Maybe to-morrow," she said.

The following morning he did not even glance at her when he saw the familiar shirt and pants on the spare bed.

" Would you like to go and look for plants in the tenantry gully? " Gip asked, with a pretence of enthusiasm.

" No, thank you," he said.

Instead he went down to the orchard and sat in the Chili-plum tree. Gip did not follow. She knew where he was and why he sat there, with his legs dangling in space as vacant as his gaze. He was out of her reach when he sat like that. Once she would have been discouraged; now she knew that he always came back. It was merely a matter of time. She wished though that she knew what shapes peopled that other world—not out of curiosity but because she could not fight unless she knew. Instead, she waited in the kitchen with Cinder until he returned, paler than ever, and the dark land of his eyes showing where " they " too waited, confident of reclaiming him.

Wednesday passed; and all that day until nightfall Gip fought with herself as a preliminary to that other fight she contemplated. Then, that night, as she sat on the edge of the bed and watched Christopher pulling on his pyjamas, she launched her attack.

" Master Christopher, I want to tell you something; but you must promise me faithfully not to tell a soul I told you. Will you promise? "

" I promise."

" Well then, come closer so nobody can hear."

She waited until Christopher stood directly in front of her, close against her knees.

" On Sunday," she began, " your mammie had a little baby. But your mammie was very ill and the baby was born dead. That was why you couldn't go to see her Sunday, and why you ain't seen her yet. But she better now, and to-morrow, God willing, maybe you can go to-morrow."

" Was it a baby boy or a baby girl? " Christopher asked. His voice was tremulous, his eyes moist and shiny. In a minute, Gip thought, the tears would flow and it would be all over. The fight would be over.

" A little boy," Gip said softly.

" A little boy? " He was scarcely audible.

He leant forward over Gip's knees until his face was

in her lap; and Gip stroked his back rhythmically, as though to smooth out its quivering with the flowing weight of her hands.

He lay there for a long time after the quivering had ceased, and he did not wake when Gip lifted him up and, staggering, carried him to bed.

Next morning Christopher found his sandals and beach-clothes waiting on the spare bed. He surveyed them expressionlessly.

" Ain't you pleased, Master Christopher? " Gip complained.

He nodded his head; but she was disappointed.

" Why you trembling so? " she asked a moment later, as she helped him on with his shorts.

" I'm not trembling," Christopher contradicted, but without the note of indignation she had expected.

For all that, as soon as he was dressed, he took up his stand outside the back door and waited anxiously for his father to appear.

" If you go on biting your nails that way," Gip told him, " you'll end up like that woman in the history book without any arms."

" I wish he would come," was all Christopher said.

That morning it seemed more than five miles to Fairmont. Christopher sat in the front seat with his father. Except once, when Ralph Stevens requested him to take his leg from under him and sit properly, there was silence. Gip watched the back of his head and wished thoughts were as discernible as fish in a glass bowl. Occasionally he looked over his shoulder at her and answered the stare with a weak smile.

She hoped he would show a little more pleasure at seeing his mother than he was showing at the prospect of it. She would tell him so too—if she got him to herself for a moment.

But there was no opportunity. As soon as they arrived, he was swallowed up by the family. Ralph Stevens went upstairs first, while Christopher swam against a tide of questions from Aunt Jessica—how his garden had fared in the rains, whether he had missed his mother, if he would be glad to go back to school. . . . Christopher had one ear listening for his father's return, and replied monosyllabically whenever possible. But his father did not return; he called Christopher from halfway down the stairs.

With knees trembling Christopher followed his father up.

" Now don't upset your mother," Ralph Stevens said over his shoulder. " She still isn't strong."

" No, sir," Christopher murmured.

He entered the bedroom on tiptoe, and crossed to the side of the bed. He stood there, looking at his mother as though glass separated them and he could do no more than press his nose against it and wish.

" You can kiss me, you know, Christopher," she laughed. Her voice startled him by its strength. He had expected a whisper, to match the face on the pillow.

He bent over and rubbed his cheek against hers.

" There's no need to be frightened," she teased him. " I won't break. I'm almost better now. It won't be long before I can go home."

Ralph Stevens was standing at the foot of the bed.

Christopher glanced nervously up at him and back at his mother. She understood the appeal.

" Leave Christopher with me for a few minutes, Ralph, dear," she said. " Francis wants to talk to you. Tell Gip to come and fetch him in a little while."

Ralph Stevens hesitated.

" Well, don't let him tire you out," he directed. As he went downstairs his footsteps echoed and fainted on silence in the room behind him.

" Well, Chris dear, what is it? " she asked.

For answer there was only a brimming of tears in Christopher's eyes, that slowly spilled over and trickled down his cheeks.

She put out her arms and Christopher threw himself between them.

" What is it, Chris dear? "

Against her shoulder she felt him trying to catch his breath for speech.

" I thought you had gone for always," he sobbed. " You said once that you were going away, and then when you went they wouldn't let me see you and they wouldn't tell me. I thought you were . . . I thought you were . . ." He paused. " And if you had, it would have been all my fault. And anyhow it's all my fault the baby died, because I put obeah on her."

Mary Stevens lifted Christopher's head off her shoulder so as to look at his face.

" What on earth are you talking about, Christopher?"

" Don't you understand either? " he said plaintively. " The new cook. She put obeah on you because I asked Rose to put it on *her*. Rose couldn't, but she did it just the same. And so the baby died and you almost did. . . ." He started to sob again.

" Christopher, my darling." She pulled him back against her and hugged him. " Is that what you thought? " She forced a laugh. " But that's all non-sense, my dear. Uncle Francis told me, years ago, when you were born, that there wouldn't be any more babies. And I was ill long before the new cook came. It was because I was ill that I fell that day. Everything went black as I was standing there talking to Old Rose."

" You mean," Christopher lifted up his head. " You mean there wouldn't have been any baby anyhow? "

She looked away from him.

" No. There wouldn't have been a baby anyhow," she said.

" Then there wasn't any obeah? " Christopher exclaimed. " And it wasn't my fault at all? "

" No, my dear. It wasn't your fault at all."

He wiped the back of his hand across his eyes.

" Only," he hesitated. " Only. You won't tell Gip about the baby, will you? Because I promised her not to say."

They were talking of other things when Gip came to fetch Christopher away.

14

It was low tide. The sea had pulled its waves away to climb some other shore, and the blue it had left behind was tremulous glass. A fisherman prowled for lobsters among the Calais reefs—a slow entertainment that did not suit Christopher's mood that morning. He ran races with his shadow in a circle around Gip.

" Can I go in, can I go in? " he yelled. " Look. There aren't any waves."

" You can paddle," Gip said severely. " Nothing more."

But paddling, like lobster-catching and looking for shells, is a sedate occupation on a morning when the sun has the sky to itself and the sea is blue glass. It was not long before Christopher tripped as he splashed in a foot of water. He showed himself to Gip.

" I fell. I'm wet all over."

" Well, you'd better get yourself dry all over before your pappy catches you," Gip told him.

" But he isn't coming," Christopher corrected her. " He's staying with Mummy. She said so."

" Well, then you can't swim. Because if you start to drown I can't get you out."

" I'll stay at the edge," he promised, " no deeper than where I was just now."

" Promise? "

" Promise."

When he tired of being alternately porpoise and turtle in twelve inches of water, he made for the casuarinas that had been uprooted in the recent high seas. It was interesting to see how quickly he could run along them without falling off into yielding dead sand. Then when he was caked all over with sand, he returned to splashing in paddle-depth. Sometimes he called out to Gip.

But Gip did not move from where she sat waiting. She just nodded her head at him and went on dreaming; because, although Christopher was in her dreams, it was not this Christopher.

Part Three: Gip

15

He played God to them: it was night when his shadow fell across the pool and day when he leant away again. The insignificant fish, sand-coloured and black, easily camouflaged themselves. He did not care about them. But there were others, angel fish with yellow moons about them, and spotted porgies. He did not particularly want to frighten these, but since they always fled before being properly seen he was forced to pursue them from one side of the pool to the other. Even that was not very satisfactory; and when he built dams of sand to contain them, they still escaped.

Sometimes he played a game of resemblances. Several of the fish looked like Uncle Francis, and occasionally he saw a rakish creature sliding by that might have been his father. But the majority were too definite in their characteristics to be identified with people. Although he would have liked to equate his mother with one of the brightly coloured ones, he could not imagine her in the guise of, say, an emperor-blue chub; or Gip—who was, anyhow, the mother of all fishes and far too large to fit into a rock pool. She sat somewhere in mid-ocean, serene among the weeds, and counted the small fry that swam past.

He wondered where Gip was. He had left her sitting under a casuarina farther up the beach, reading her prayer book. She was always reading her prayer book —now even more than before. He thought she should know it all by heart after so many readings. Prayers were not, of course, very easy to learn by heart. They didn't rhyme; and they contained big broad words like sin, majesty, power and glory; there was nothing to grasp, nothing to remember. The few that he knew were repeated automatically at bedtime. He mouthed the sounds without trying to understand what it was they signified. Gip seemed quite happy about that; and if, during the day, she scolded him, she never invoked anything more incomprehensible than just plain God. God didn't like this and God didn't like that. . . . He was difficult to please but at least His likes and dislikes were definite.

But he wished, anyhow, that Gip wouldn't read her prayers so much. It was awfully dull and made him feel that he should talk in whispers.

On that thought Christopher opened his mouth and gave a loud war-whoop before rushing up the beach to the casuarina tree.

" That's a dreadful sound, Master Chris," Gip admonished him. " You frightened the book out of my hands."

Christopher laughed.

" You must have been asleep."

" When you get as old as me you'll doze off too. All this heat," she grumbled.

" It's the prayers," Christopher contradicted. " They make me sleepy in church sometimes."

" Well, the Lord won't be at all pleased if you go to sleep in church. That's the one place you shouldn't."

" How do you know He wouldn't? You always say that, but I don't see how you know. Nobody can talk to Him; you told me so yourself."

" You growing to be a most contradictorious young boy," Gip informed him. " Anyway, when I ever said you couldn't talk to Him? You read your New Testament stories, don't you? The disciples used to talk to Him."

" But that was long ago," Christopher pointed out. " And in any case that was before they crucified Him."

" Makes no difference. And not only does He *hear* what you say "—Gip jabbed a finger at him, to emphasise and to warn—"but He even sees what you *think*. So you be careful now."

Christopher had no response for that. He ran off down the beach again, slowing as his thoughts caught up with him. He imagined himself thinking " That red-faced old fish looks like Uncle Francis," and saw the thought float out on the air above him, enclosed in a balloon. That, at least, was how it was done in the picture books. Then the balloon exploded, and the letters rained down upon him.

" That's silly," he told himself. But he was not altogether convinced.

" But does God," he asked Gip later, " listen all the time? "

" Course not. He don't bother to listen to everything. He wouldn't listen, for instance, when you talk about what things you find on the beach this morning. But

He listening now because we talking about Him; and He always listens when you talk *to* Him."

" You mean," Christopher suggested, " that if I said I'd found a sea slug this morning as big as this "—he held his arms apart—" then God wouldn't hear? "

" I don't mean that at all, Master Christopher. If you tell a fib He'll certainly hear it and write it all down. That's why I always warning you not to."

Christopher pouted.

" Well, I don't see how He can know it's not true if He isn't listening."

" It's like I told you," Gip explained patiently. " He don't have to listen all the time; but when you tell a lie it's like . . . it's like if your words was a great red fire coming out of your mouth. And then He listens because He can see it's a lie."

Christopher lapsed into silence in order to contemplate his recent fibs. They were not, in fact, very numerous—chiefly because there was nobody who was likely to be taken in by them. Playtime at school provided the only real opportunity. He had, for example, claimed possession of a huge old book, so tattered that he could never actually produce it for the other boys to see, in which was described every sort of game ever invented or imagined. Most of the games to which he introduced his confrères belonged, in fact, to the second category. Devised in his own imagination, they were presented with the authoritative backing of the *Book of Games*. This was almost sufficient in itself to warrant their success; if, on the other hand, they failed, he was not to be held responsible, except in so far as he might have forgotten some essential detail in the rules.

Sometimes he found the weight of the *Book of Games* quite intolerable. All other fibs were a once-only; but this one lasted for ever. New games were always in demand, and his imagination sorely taxed on occasion. He had thought of mislaying the book or having it stolen, even of confessing its non-existence. But its possession gave him a certain authority, and he was not sure of his ability to stand without it. If he confessed, Ronnie, who had all kinds of lurid information about why girls differed from boys and how babies were made, would certainly assume the leadership—or even Peter. Peter was almost too fat to run, and spattered you with saliva when he spoke; on the other hand he had a stepfather—his own had cut his throat—and he lived in town and went to the cinema every Saturday.

Christopher considered his own resources. There was the garden; but none of the boys was interested in gardening. There were the animals; but none of the animals at Surrey-house seemed to do the peculiar things that, according to Ronnie, the animals pastured on the racecourse indulged in. Even his occasional visits to Fairmont were not news, since both Ronnie and the new boy who had come last term went regularly to the Aquatic Club with their parents, and were allowed to dive and swim a long way out by themselves.

Christopher sighed. He couldn't, he concluded, do without the *Book of Games* just yet. He must first of all find something to take its place. Perhaps Best, who knew a lot about what animals did, would help him. It was no use asking Gip. She had been horrified merely because he had once remarked that Uncle Francis's sow looked large enough to have a litter of at least ten. Certainly he didn't believe any of what Ronnie had said about how piglets were made. He had had to pretend, of course, that he knew it all already. Anyhow, it didn't matter, Best would put him right; and he would then be able to confound Ronnie on his own ground.

But Best, as it turned out, had no intention of being co-operative.

" Why you don't ask your mammy," he said, " or your school mistress? You go to school, don't you? "

" They don't teach us *that* at school," Christopher told him crossly. " And Mummy won't tell me."

" Did you ever ask her? "

" Of course I did. She said Daddy would tell me . . ." —he paused and kicked a pebble embedded in the ground, adding scornfully, ". . . when I am old enough."

Best laughed and returned to kneading his cotton-seed cakes.

" Any little nigger boy in the yard can tell you," he said over his shoulder. " Any little nigger boy your own age who don't go to school."

" Well, I certainly won't ask *them*," Christopher informed him defiantly.

He aimed another kick at the pebble. It still did not move. Best only laughed.

He certainly had no intention of asking one of the yard boys. Such a question would evidence a far

greater degree of intimacy than he was willing to accord
any of them. In particular, he resented the suggestion that they knew already although some of them
were no older than he was and didn't go to school
regularly.

16

When Christopher went out again after breakfast, he found a ladder propped against the west wall of the house. This, he knew, could only mean one thing. On the roof at Surrey-house was a large rain-water tank, big as a swimming-pool. It was not visible from the ground since it lay below the level of the other roofs in order to gather the rain that drained off them. Periodically—about once a year—the outlet to the tank became so clogged with fallen leaves that all the water had to be bailed out and the inside of the tank scraped and cleaned. For this purpose a thirty-foot ladder was propped against the parapet and a gang of men, bare-footed and armed with buckets, climbed up. They threw the water over the side, clean at first and then thicker and thicker with rotted leaves, until the ground below looked as if it had been plastered with brown paint.

It had long been Christopher's ambition to watch this performance from a ringside seat—standing, for preference, in the water itself. It would be even better, of course, if he were allowed to bathe in the tank before it was cleaned. That was the most satisfactory way of having a bath that he could imagine, particularly as the

water, at this time of day at any rate, would be warm
with the morning's sunshine.

Seeing the ladder, Christopher only hesitated long
enough to calculate his chances of being observed. His
parents would be safe indoors, resting as usual after
breakfast, and the workmen would soon be going home
for their midday meal as well. Obviously they would
not start work now, before they went—which gave him
at least a couple of hours with the tank to himself.

Accustomed as he was to tree-climbing, the ladder
held no terrors. At the top, though, there was a
problem. The ladder was not quite long enough, and
above the last rung was an empty space of wall that had
somehow to be scaled. However, he found that by
standing on tiptoe he could just reach the inside edge
of the parapet and pull himself up.

The whitewash felt chalky under his hands and the
soles of his feet started to itch. It was an unpleasant
sensation, one that he had never been able to understand. There seemed to be no connection between the
feel of chalk and one's feet. But from past experience
he knew what the next stage would be. His fingers
would begin to swell, and then it would be difficult to
take his weight on them. Grasping the wall decisively,
he heaved his chest on to the parapet. Then, gripping
sideways with one knee, he prised the rest of his body
up.

For a moment he lay still, looking down. Essie came
out of the kitchen door immediately below and he had
to resist the temptation to drop a ball of spit on the step
beside her. She could not see him from where she stood,

but it was better to take no chances. He could hear her grumbling to someone inside.

" What they left this ladder here for? Only for people to trip over and break their neck."

She shook out a cloth and went back indoors. Christopher crawled along the parapet to the point where the roof sloped below it. From the edge of the roof it was only a step into the tank; but for the moment he satisfied himself with sitting on the hot shingles and dangling his feet in the water. It was deliciously tepid. There didn't seem to be very many leaves, though, not nearly enough to require cleaning out. But the workmen probably didn't know that yet. Perhaps they wouldn't bother to do it after all—which meant that before long he might have another opportunity for visiting the tank.

The roofs over the main body of the building were arranged in three peaks, with gutters between them, slightly tilted so as to conduct the water into the tank. By crawling along the edge of the roof he was on, it was possible for Christopher to reach the vee between it and the second roof. He could then walk along the gutter to the edge of the house on the far side. Since he had plenty of time, this seemed quite a worthwhile first project. It also proved to be a great deal easier than it looked. The wooden shingles offered a good grip to the soles of his feet and, in spite of the slope of the roof, he was able to move quite quickly, without fear of sliding crab-wise into the tank.

The roof-high panorama on the other side of the house was far more surprising than he had anticipated. When he climbed to the top of the mango tree in the orchard, there were always leaves to prevent him seeing out; anyhow, the orchard was in a hollow of land, far below the level of the house. From here, on the other hand, he could see everything spread out like a pattern on a carpet. The long bed immediately below seemed, with its rows of different-coloured shrubs, much neater than from ground-level. The dwarf casuarinas along the drive all appeared to be the same size, shape, and distance apart; and the drive swept in a neat grey ribbon between the triangle of turf on one side and the rectangle of lawn on the other. Christopher closed his eyes and with one finger mapped out the details on the air. Once they were fixed in his mind he could transfer them to paper later. He did not quite know how he would explain a drawing made from so singular an angle of vision, but he would worry about that when he had done it. At the moment the most important thing was a swim in the tank. The sun beat straight down on the roof and the metal of the gutter stung through the callouses on his soles. Briefly he debated whether it was really safe to take off his clothes. If any-thing happened, it would be difficult to put them on again in a hurry. On the other hand, it was hardly sufficient to have come this far, and at such risk, merely in order to paddle.

He splashed around the tank for about half an hour, at first with pleasure and then because he thought it should be giving him pleasure. In fact, it wasn't. There was nothing to see but the sides of the tank, the roof and the naked sky. The water was too shallow for proper swimming, and so lifeless, clinging and warm that he felt more tired than exhilarated. He climbed out and sat waiting dejectedly for the sun to dry him; and once he was dressed, he scarcely spared another glance for the scene around him. He crawled back along the parapet to the ladder.

The ladder, however, was not there.

When his heart had returned to a more normal pulse, and he had stifled the vision—and the trembling that went with it—of what would have happened if, confident of finding the ladder beneath him, he had launched himself over the side without looking, Christopher began to consider what he should do. For a few minutes he lay quietly, not really thinking, but speculating in a kind of half-dream whether Essie might still be in the kitchen and, if so, whether she would hear if he called. He leaned over the edge, and eventually, summoning up his courage, uttered the kind of suppressed shout that he thought might reach her in the kitchen but not his parents on the other side of the house.

" Essie."

No one came. The air buzzed with that even sound of noonday heat like innumerable wings. He tried again, a little louder.

" Essie."

He began to grow dizzy with looking down. The heat rose to meet him in transparent spirals, tangling in his eyes. Better not stay here, he thought; if he became giddy, he would fall off.

Back on the edge of the roof Christopher calculated the possibilities. Either the workmen were going to clean the tank, in which case they would bring the ladder back and would find him on the roof; or they had already been up and had decided that the job didn't need doing. It was just possible, in either case, that all was not lost. His father didn't always supervise the workmen and he, Christopher, might persuade them not to give him away. On the other hand, if they did not return he would have to attract somebody's attention and get the ladder brought back. He might manage that too without his father knowing. But both were equally unlikely—and anyhow he would have to wait till afternoon came and work started again in the house and yard.

Or suppose he didn't let anyone know that he was on the roof? Probably no one would notice till dinner-time, and then when he still didn't come, they would start frantically searching—in the orchard, by the pond, perhaps even in the tenantry gully. Perhaps if he didn't show himself until they were really worried they would be so relieved at finding him that he wouldn't be caned or even scolded. It would be a long wait though, and it wasn't as if there was anything interesting to do in the meantime. He didn't want to swim any more . . . and when the sun started to go down it would be very eerie. He certainly couldn't wait until the sun went down, because then he wouldn't be able to move at all for fear of falling in the tank, or, worse, over the parapet. He shivered at the prospect as though a cold finger of night had already touched his spine.

He tried to think of something else.

Where did the rats live that he sometimes heard at night scampering around the roof? At least, Gip said they were rats; he'd never been too sure. What was there for rats to eat up here? Unless they ate one another, of course. They would probably eat him too if they found him trespassing in their domain after dark —as they ate that man in the poem who kept all the corn. He could always stand in the middle of the tank; they probably wouldn't brave the water in order to get at him. But he wouldn't be able to stand in the water all night either. . . .

About an hour later Christopher heard movement in the yard below. It sounded as if someone had brought back the ladder and was propping it against the wall. The workmen! They were going to clean the tank after all. The point was, should he wait for them to come up and find him or should he go to meet them? Perhaps it would be better if he did something, pretended to be enjoying himself, so that they wouldn't think that he was worried or penitent.

He quickly installed himself on the edge of the roof, dangled his feet in the water, and splashed vigorously. A head appeared over the edge of the parapet. It was Donald's. Christopher was so surprised that he forgot to splash. Donald certainly wouldn't be coming to clean the tank. . . .

"You got to come down now, Master Chris," Donald said.

Christopher gaped at him.

"How did you know I was here? "

Donald did not look at him. "The master told me to fetch you down, that's all."

Christopher's heart sank. He did not bother to ask

how his father had known; he just followed Donald down the ladder.

" I suppose," he said, when they reached the bottom, " he wants to see me? "

" In the office, Master Chris."

As he turned away Donald gave him a playful slap on the behind. Christopher did not know whether it was meant as affection or warning, but he ignored it. Head down he went up the stairs to his father's office.

Ralph Stevens did not look up when Christopher appeared in the doorway. He seemed to be adding a column of figures. Christopher hesitated. Perhaps it was all part of the punishment. He, however, was anxious to get the business over and done with.

" Donald says you want me," he said.

Ralph Stevens did not turn.

" Yes," he drawled absentmindedly. " Did you enjoy yourself on the roof, Christopher? "

Christopher was familiar with the technique. It was the way Boodles played with a mouse. He did not bother to answer.

" You must be careful next time not to walk in the gutters. They're not very strong, you know. Besides, you can be heard in the rooms below."

A sudden thought struck Christopher. Listlessness fell away as anger flushed into his cheeks.

" Was it you who had the ladder taken away then? " he burst out; and by his father's grim little laugh he knew that he had guessed correctly. " Suppose I hadn't looked? " he raged. " I nearly didn't too. . . ."

But he was trembling so much that he couldn't continue.

Ralph Stevens looked at him.

" So you got a fright as well? " he said. " Perhaps then, you won't do it again." He turned back to his books, but only momentarily. When he swivelled round in his chair, both his face and his tone had lost their coolness. " And if," he thundered, " you hadn't once before had sunstroke I would have kept you there till midnight. Now go to your room and stay there till I tell you you can leave."

Christopher went. To a certain extent his father's rage had cut his own from beneath him. Only the trembling remained, that and a feeling of small-ness. He was almost glad that Gip was ill and would not be waiting for him in his bedroom. He suspected that this was one occasion when she might not be sym-pathetic.

But why? And why should he feel small into the bargain? His father had done a beastly thing, and he might have broken his neck. He rather wished that he had. At least then his father, not he, would be in the wrong.

He went and sat on the window-sill, unsuccessfully trying to argue himself into anger once more. If only his father had caned him!

Outside the sun blazed on, unconcerned about any part it might have played in the day's events. The pale green scent of ginger-lilies hung on the air, heavy as the heat. The casuarinas that lined the drive were no longer neat, identical shapes. Christopher fetched his drawing book and began to depict them in the round symmetry they had assumed from above, with a rectangle of lawn beyond and a triangle of grass on the near side.

At least he wouldn't have to find any excuse now for the peculiar picture that this would turn out to be.

17

THE GAPS between Gip's illnesses had grown shorter and shorter. At one point she had even suggested that Mrs. Stevens find someone else to look after Christopher because she did not think she would be able to continue working. But Christopher had reacted to that suggestion with such a display of temper that Mary Stevens had never dared broach the subject to her husband. Contemplation blanched at the vision of scenes that would result if Ralph decided on a replacement and Christopher carried out his threats of rebelliousness.

" I won't do anything she says," he had threatened, and followed this negative declaration with a long affirmation of what he would do, ending up, " Besides, I don't need a nanny any more."

Mary Stevens left it at that, employed a girl in the kitchen for half a day and handed over more and more of Gip's work to Cinder. This was not much of a transition since Gip's burdens had in any case grown lighter as Christopher had grown older. Christopher, too, was accustomed to Cinder. She had been with the family as long as he could remember himself. But even so, Mary Stevens thought her son should be prepared for the fact that in life scenes cannot always be as un-changing as he appeared to imagine.

Death, she found—for some reason which she did not stop to analyse—came more easily to her tongue in talking to him than birth ever had.

" Have you ever stopped to think," she concluded, " how old Gip is? "

" She's not as old as Rose," Christopher replied. " She told me so. Nor as old as Grandfather."

" Well, *they* won't live for ever either, you know."

Christopher thought for a moment. He did not like the discussion and wished his mother had not started it. He turned restlessly on one foot.

" Anyhow, she's not going to die," he declared.

But it was simpler to leave his mother than to leave the subject, and doubt tangled with conviction in his final words, delivered from the doorway.

" God won't let her."

He was not, in fact, at all certain about God. He couldn't, in the first place, remember any occasion when he had prayed to God and had his wish granted. Gip said that was because he didn't pray hard enough. In that case he didn't expect ever to succeed. But far more important was the fact that Gip did not really seem to want to live. On more than one occasion he had heard her say to Cinder or Essie, as she bemoaned her rheumatics: " Every day I pray to the good Lord to take me." And if Gip was praying to die and he was praying for her not to, he had no doubt as to who would be successful. There was that big lie of his about

the *Book of Games* which made it altogether unlikely that
God would listen to him.

Without having chosen any particular direction for
his footsteps, Christopher found himself in the back
yard on the way to the servants' quarters. He stopped
outside Gip's door and listened. There was a monotonous sound of someone mumbling, which meant that
she wasn't asleep but was either reading the Bible or
saying her prayers. For a moment Christopher's good
intentions left him. He picked up a stone and threw it
peevishly at the henhouse. Why was she always reading
the Bible and praying? And why did she always shut
up her room so tightly that the sun and wind couldn't
get in? Inside it was dark, and the air was heavy with
some indefinable but faintly cloying sweetness. It was
like the air in church. It was air that seemed to be
trying to suck one's life away.

People should go to church outdoors, as Cinder did.
And once a year they all went to the beach and danced
around a white sheet. Every time they passed the priest
on their way around they dropped a penny on the sheet.
Then when the priest thought he had enough pennies,
he took the congregation down to the surf and ducked
them all in turn in the sea. That was supposed to wash
away their wickedness; but even if it didn't at least they
enjoyed themselves doing it.

It wouldn't be right, though, to duck Gip in the sea.
The waves would probably topple her over and hurt
her; and if they didn't she would certainly catch
her death of cold as she was always threatening *he*
would.

Christopher sighed. He threw another stone at the

henhouse—one that reached its target in a parabola instead of a petulant straight line—and knocked.

" Can I come in? " he asked.

" The door open," Gip answered. " Just push it."

It was dark inside, as he had expected, so he left the door ajar. The grass mattress hissed comfortingly as he settled himself on the edge of the bed. He wondered fleetingly whether it might not be the grass that gave the room its peculiar sweet smell.

" Don't you feel any better? " he inquired hopefully.

" I ain't too bad, Master Chris. It comes and goes, you know. And what you been doing? "

" Wouldn't you like the shutters open a little? " he asked. " You'll hurt your eyes if you read in here."

" I wasn't reading," Gip sighed. " Just saying my prayers. I don't feel like reading. All those letters make my poor head spin. But tell me: what you been doing? "

" Oh nothing. I drew a picture for Miss May." He shot a glance at Gip out of the corner of his eye. . . . But she would hear anyhow, he concluded—if she hadn't heard already. " I couldn't come to see you yesterday because I went up on the roof after breakfast and Daddy made Donald take the ladder away and when Donald put it back Daddy sent me inside and I had to stay there till dinner-time."

" Donald told me," Gip said quietly. She took one of his hands in hers and, alternately patting and rubbing it, seemed to be trying to massage into him an understanding of what she was saying. " You mustn't do these things, Master Chris. How many times I tell you you mustn't be disobedient, nor reckless, nor foolish, nor vex your pappy? Please the Lord I won't be here too much longer. But I won't go in peace if I ain't sure you'll be behaving yourself. You can promise me to behave yourself, Master Chris? "

" But you aren't going to die," Christopher told her vehemently. " I've prayed that you won't die and you won't! "

Gip laughed, but her eyes shone wet. Christopher looked away quickly for fear of what his own might do.

" You mustn't pray for things like that, Master Chris. Even Jesus when he prayed said, ' But Thy will, O Father, be done.' It's for Him to decide, not we."

" But *you* pray to die," he accused her. " I've heard you tell Cinder that you pray every night to die."

" I pray," she admitted sadly. " I pray. But the good Lord knows what I mean. I'm not asking Him to take me before He's ready, only to receive me when He is." She paused. When she went on it was more in the tone of prayer than of explanation. " I only pray He won't let me suffer too long." Then, remembering Christopher, she added, " Just as I pray every day that He give you His guidance and not let you stumble. You must pray for that too. Only He can help you."

Christopher grimaced. He was embarrassed. Gip sensed it and changed her tone.

" But what you doing cooped up in a sick room when the sun shining outside? " she bustled. " You get your-self off, Master Chris. Tell Cinder to take you in the gully and bring me back a bunch of sage flowers like

the last time. And ask Cinder to pull some fresh senna
leaves for me," she called after him as he shut the door
behind him.

Christopher did not immediately go in search of
Cinder. Behind the servants' quarters lay the orchard,
and by crawling along a drain it was possible to arrive
there without detour. The drain was not particularly
savoury. It led, in fact, to the cesspool, where the
washings from the pigsties were also collected, to serve
as a reservoir of liquid manure for the citrus trees. It
was something of a test, however, to see whether one
could get through the drain without wetting one's feet
in the trickle of bilge that coursed down its middle and
without drawing a single breath of the noisome air that
hung over the damp stones. That achieved, one's chest
exploded with the effort, and gulped back a lungful of
the even more noisome cesspool air. But beyond the
cesspool were the lime trees with their clean, astringent
smell, the chance of ripe guavas, and, finally, right at
the back, under the cliff that was also a wall, the most
challenging tree in the orchard. It was an avocado that
grew straight up, regular, and with the rough bark that
makes most avocados things of scorn for the true tree-
climber. The challenge of this particular tree lay in the
fact that one branch, too narrow for crawling on and
with no parallel growth above it to cling to, pushed out
over the wall. It was possible, by hanging on the
branch and moving out along its length a hand at a
time, to reach the cliff and land on it. Then, via the
cow-shed, one could return to the house without even
appearing to have been in the orchard.

Christopher's mastery of this particular tree was a recent achievement. No one had been told, as the Tarzan device would certainly have been disapproved of in the strongest terms. He was not forbidden to go into the orchard, so that a secret exit was not really called for. That it was unnecessary, however, constituted part of its charm. He imagined occasions when, running away from home, or pursued by bandits who had murdered all his family, he disappeared into the night without trace.

Cinder was not enthusiastic about the tenantry gully. " That nasty stinking place," she exclaimed when Christopher broached the subject.

As usual, however, he prevailed, though none of the arguments he used—particularly the one about "perhaps seeing a monkey"—was of the kind likely to persuade her.

" Gip doesn't like the gully either," he confessed when they were well on their way. " Why? "

" Because it dark and wet," Cinder declared feelingly.

" Not in the daytime," he protested. " Anyhow, it's because it's wet that so many interesting things grow there."

" That may be. But you better watch where you put your feet. They don't have no closets in the tenantry like we got at Surrey-house. . . . And that ain't all either," she added ominously under her breath.

" Why, what else is there? " Christopher wanted to know. But it was apparent from her padlocked look that she had no intention of explaining. " Is it because of obeah? " he suggested in a mock-awed voice.

" Obeah, Master Chris? " Cinder laughed. " Something a sight more natural than obeah, I can tell you." She stopped to face him, arms akimbo. " For why you always so interested in obeah? " she demanded. " You don't know them things best left alone? Obeah! " she repeated scornfully.

A hedge of wild agaves marked the spot where the land gaped to form a sudden ravine. They grew along both cliffs and fenced the gully as effectively as barbed wire. Only here and there was the line incomplete, indicating that a path of sorts led downwards.

Leaving the road, Cinder and Christopher had to walk a long way before they came to an opening. The cart-track meandered between a wall of full-grown sugar cane on one side and the palisade of agaves on the other. Progress was rendered even slower by Christopher's search among the spears and spines of the agaves for those on which he had written his name last time he visited the gully. In addition, he had to write his name on several more. This was done by twisting the nib-like point off the end of one withered frond and pressing with it on the tough green skin of another. Enough force had to be exerted to break the skin, so that the leaf bled its aloe-thin sap into the wounds. These then dried in the sunlight, and one's name remained, a calligraphic scab, engraved on the leaf until it, in its turn, withered.

Christopher was not the only one who used the agaves for his scribbles. The other entries were more often, however, in the form of etchings than letters—he presumed because very few of the boys in the village could write. These drawings had to be inspected surreptitiously. Cinder did not approve of them at all —which was a pity because he did not always understand what they were supposed to represent and she might have been able to tell him. In most cases, it was fairly obvious what the artists had in mind, even though nobody, Christopher was sure, was made as some of the drawings showed them. They wouldn't be able to walk if they were.

" Come along, Master Christopher," Cinder snapped on one occasion when he lingered longer than usual. " That ain't nothing for you to be looking at, I sure."

Christopher blushed.

" How do you know? " he said. " I don't see anything."

" Well maybe that's just as well."

They reached a gap in the hedge of agaves, and Christopher rushed on ahead. Cinder yelled after him.

" Careful. You'll fall."

Christopher paid no attention, and was already bent double in a clump of ferns by the time she arrived at the bottom.

" We forgot to bring anything to take plants back in," he complained. " And I've already found a fern."

" You know ferns don't grow when you move them —particularly from this wet ground."

" I've grown lots of ferns from down here," he contradicted hotly.

" You've got plenty anyhow. What we came for is sage and senna leaves . . . and I don't want to spend more of the afternoon in this gully than I can help."

She sniffed the air and looked around her disparagingly. But in spite of this prologue they spent
nearly an hour. There was always, according to
Christopher, something just ahead that had to be
examined more closely. Occasionally the " something"
existed: more often than not it was just a patch of
darker green or a suggestion of colour. There was
actually little by way of colour—a periwinkle, a four
o'clock, a sage bush in bloom. But the greens were
intense: the shadows themselves were green-black like
trampled lichen, and the air palely tinted.

When they climbed up out of the gully they found
themselves near the main road and almost a mile from
home. Cinder's apron was laden with a variety of
plants, and Christopher carried a calabash with as
much pride as if it were the royal orb that it resembled.

" That's the farthest I've ever been in the gully," he
announced, " and, you see, nothing happened."

" What you did expect to happen, Master Christopher? " Cinder asked in amazement.

" It was you who said it, not me," he protested.
" You said the tenantry used it as a W.C. and that
other things happened too. Don't you remember? "

" Yes, I remember."

Christopher thought for a moment.

" Is it the drawings you mean? " he asked finally.

" It ain't the drawings, Master Christopher, though
they is bad enough. And don't ask me no questions 'cos
I ain't going to give you no answers."

Christopher sighed. Whatever she might say, he was
sure it had something to do with the drawings. Perhaps
there really were men with long things between their

legs like snakes; maybe they hid in the gully at night and frightened people who went down there because there were no toilets in the tenantry.

He smiled at the thought. It was a most unlikely explanation but quite amusing to contemplate.

18

Apart from the fernery and the centre of the orchard there was only one spot at Surrey-house that was damp and shady enough for growing plants that had come from the tenantry gully. This was a hollow of land near the pond. Sheltered on two sides by cliffs and on the third by a monstrous hog-plum tree, it was the second of Christopher's special preserves. In importance, however, it ranked far below his triangular garden. Too far from the house, it was melancholy both by nature and by reason of the use to which it was put. It was, in fact, the pets' cemetery; and though certain plants flourished there, they were all what Christopher classed in his mind as " graveyard plants "—eucharist lilies, tuberoses, and dark-leaved coleus. A huge-trumpeted convolvulus, of the kind invariably grown over outhouse lavatories, clambered up the face of one cliff. In the crevices of the other Christopher had planted wild maidenhair ferns as far up as he could reach. On its two open sides the precincts of the grove were marked out with clumps of an iris-leaved perennial that had never flowered and had, as far as he knew, no name. He was always hoping to be surprised one day by a sudden explosion of blossom, exotic as the occasional blooms on the cacti that Aunt Margaret so loved. But the clumps seemed to expend all their energy in multiplying sideways, so that he frequently had to dig them up and thin them out. This was almost the only chore that the cemetery imposed upon him. Otherwise it was merely a case of keeping the place tidy, seeing that the stones which marked the graves did not become overgrown and, very occasionally, putting in some new plants culled from the gully.

There had been no time when they returned from the gully to rearrange the pets' cemetery so as to accommodate the new acquisitions. The plants had therefore been left in water, while Christopher took his collection of sage flowers for Gip and Cinder made senna tea. Early next morning Christopher loaded the plants in the wheelbarrow and trundled it through the yard, past the cow-shed, and over the crest of the hill to the pond. He passed Best on the way but did not stop to talk. Best still refused to tell him what he wanted to know so he didn't see any reason why he should waste time being friendly.

Under the hog-plum tree dew lay on the grass. The cold drops trickled off on Christopher's arms as he set about discarding and transplanting to make space for the new arrivals. It was a clammy job, all the more so because of the number of spider's threads that floated on the air. They tangled about his nostrils and when he tried to remove them his fingers left a smear of wet mud in their place. He was glad when Oslin arrived to interrupt him.

" Master Chris," Oslin began, his foolish face even more foolish with the huge grin of some private joke,

" Best tell you if you want to know what it is you ask him about, go in the flue-house. But he say don't let your pappy see. He in the yard by the cow-shed."

There was no difficulty, as Oslin knew, about getting into the flue-house without being seen. Originally designed for curing tobacco, the building was now half a ruin. The space formerly occupied by the furnaces was a tangle of rusty metal, and at the chimney foot was a hole large enough for a man to climb through. Nothing but old lumber was kept in the flue-house, and though the door was padlocked it was so rotten and chinky that it would have collapsed at a push. Since the building abutted the cow-shed at right angles one could, through the crevices, command a view of almost the entire yard.

With Oslin leading the way Christopher circled the pond and climbed up the slope behind the cow-shed. On hands and knees they crawled through the hole in the chimney and into the flue-house. It was dark inside.

" Are there any fortylegs? " Christopher asked nervously.

" They always some," Oslin whispered back. " But only in the lumber."

Giving the stacks of wood a wide berth, Christopher made for the door. The light shining through the crevices restored his confidence a little, but he could not help wondering what would happen if a fortyleg bit him and he revealed his presence by screaming.

Outside a small group was gathered around Maisie the Jersey milch-cow. She was tied to a post with her head down. Ralph Stevens was issuing instructions, though for the moment nothing appeared to be happening. Then Best and Frank came out of the cow-shed leading Burn between them. Burn was a handsome Zebu bull, with a massive hump between his shoulders and a malevolent gleam in his eyes. He was always penned alone because of his uncertain temper. For once he seemed fairly tractable; but even so there were two ropes through his nose-ring, both held short by the cowmen. As they led Burn up to where Maisie stood, Best handed his rope to another man. The bull snorted and tossed his head; but he made no attempt to use his horns when the two men lengthened their hold on the ropes.

For a moment Christopher glanced down to make sure that there was no fortyleg circling his foot. At an exclamation from Oslin he looked up again.

" He up now," Oslin commented with satisfaction.

Christopher did not immediately understand what had happened. Burn, it seemed, had attacked Maisie. Then, as he took in the immobility of the scene, and realised that it was by design that Burn was now crouched over Maisie's back, a phrase of Ronnie's flashed through his mind. He rejected it with a shudder, as he had at the time.

" The foolish bull! " Oslin made a disparaging noise. " Best going have to put it in for him."

Christopher drew in his breath, stiffening. As Best moved towards Burn, a kind of dread rivetted his gaze to the bull's hindquarters. He felt sure that he would cry out; but his heart was in his throat, choking all sound. He saw Best grasp the bull's penis and direct it.

Then the breath he had held so long exploded, and a thin, high whine quivered through him. He turned and ran.

Christopher did not appear when the breakfast gong sounded at eleven o'clock. Nor was he to be found in any of his usual hideouts. However, his absence was more a cause for annoyance than alarm. There were many places where he might be, out of hearing of the house and with only his stomach to indicate the passage of time.

The Stevenses finished their meal and the servants theirs.

" Where you suppose that boy-child is? " Cinder complained as she helped Essie with the last of the dishes.

" I can't keep the stove in any longer," Essie told her, " or the firewood won't last—and the mistress always ready to say I taking it home. He'll have to eat cold food."

" The master done say he ain't to have no food if he can't come in time."

" What you keeping it for then? " Essie teased.

Christopher did not return until much later. The yard was empty and the household resting. Cinder waited, dozing on the kitchen bench. She knew he would have to come in through the kitchen, since the back door was bolted when the Stevenses retired for their afternoon siesta, and the front of the house was never open at this time of day. However, she did not hear him enter. He was already halfway up the stairs when their creaking woke her.

" Master Christopher," she called after him angrily. " What you mean by creeping in like that? Just you come back here this minute, sir."

Christopher stopped but did not turn.

" You heard me, Master Christopher? " Cinder threatened.

He eyed her over one shoulder. Seeing the expression on her face, he decided to obey, and turned back.

" Lord! " Cinder threw her hands in the air in horror. " What you been doing to get in that state? "

" Nothing," he mumbled.

" How you mean ' nothing,' Master Chris? Both your knees covered in blood and your face all scratched. What you been doing, child? "

Christopher hesitated.

" I was in the canes," he said finally.

But that didn't explain the bruises on his knees where he had cut himself as he retreated too precipitously through the hole in the flue-house wall.

" I fell down," he added.

" Anybody with half an eye can see you fell down," Cinder commented acidly. " But how? Those cuts ain't nothing fresh. You ain't just got them. And look at the time." She pointed to the clock at the head of the stairs. " Breakfast been over nigh two hours and you only now come in, and blood all over you. What your pappy going say? " She lowered her voice and repeated. " What your pappy going say? "

Christopher did not reply. He stared without expression, as though waiting for her to calm down and tell him what he was supposed to do. Cinder glared back. But eventually it was she who gave in.

" Come on," she snatched his hand and hustled him towards the stairs. " We got to wash them cuts—and," she added, with a final show of wrath like the splutter of a dying firework, " with iodine. Though you probably got them infected already."

19

NOBODY EVER discovered where Christopher had been that morning. Ralph Stevens tried first. He always had his siesta in his bedroom, reclining in a Berbice chair with his legs stretched out along its arms. When Cinder brought in the tea tray at two o'clock he sent her to summon Christopher.

" Why were you late for breakfast? " he asked.

Christopher dropped his eyes.

" I went too far in the canes," he murmured, " and I couldn't find the way out."

" That doesn't sound very plausible," Ralph Stevens remarked dryly. " However, we'll let it pass this time. But don't let it happen again.'

Christopher did not move.

" Kindly look at me when I'm speaking to you," Ralph Stevens snapped, " and not at the floor."

Christopher blushed furiously. He suddenly realised that his eyes had been fixed on his father's open fly-buttons.

" Did you hear what I said, Christopher? "

" Yes, sir," he said. " I'm not to go in the canes again."

Ralph Stevens looked at him curiously. Noticing it, Christopher's gaze fell again.

" All right, you may go."

Mary Stevens was no more successful in her attempts. Worse than that, she sensed something new and un- pleasant in Christopher's attitude, almost akin to antipathy. He gave the same explanation in almost the same words that she had heard him use to his father. When she cajoled and put an arm around him, he suffered the embrace as coldly as a gargoyle and dis- entangled himself at the first sign of a let-up in the questioning.

Whether or not Christopher had been all that time in a cane field and why, anyhow, he should have gone into a cane field, which offered no kind of entertain- ment except that of battling with sword-edged leaves and the itchy down of fallen trash, were perhaps not questions of a vital importance. It was only Christo- pher's mode of reply that invested them with signifi- cance. He did not appear to be lying, but he was certainly concealing. Mary Stevens was perturbed. For the life of her she could not imagine what might have happened. Had he fought with one of the yard boys? Had he fallen out of one of the trees he was always climbing? . . . But neither seemed to explain the chilliness of his behaviour, the resentment to questions.

There was only one person in whom Christopher was likely to confide. Pensively she made her way to the servants' quarters.

Gip had never believed in making conversational detours with Christopher; and this, she judged, was no moment in her life to start. Nevertheless, when she saw

Christopher next morning, resolution wavered. Watching him as he nestled into the side of the bed, she began to doubt whether she would ask any of the relevant questions.

" You ain't got fever, Master Chris, have you? " she said, taking his hand. " You look to me as if you sickening for something."

" I'm not sick," he contradicted. " It's you who's sick. Are you going to be better by next Sunday? We're going to the sea next Sunday."

Gip pretended to laugh.

" If I can hold these bones together long enough to get there," she said, " I think I'd be better off at church next Sunday."

" No, don't go to church," Christopher pleaded. "You've been saying so many prayers, you don't need to go to church. Besides, you haven't been to the sea for a long time now—and you said yourself that the sea air is good for your rheumatism."

" Well, we'll see what the good Lord allows." She hesitated. " And what you been up to? "

She spoke in a matter-of-fact way, taking the precaution of looking down as she spoke. She felt Christopher's eyes sweep over hers like the turning beam of a lighthouse.

" Nothing much," he said. " This morning I painted. Yesterday I planted out the plants I found in the gully. But the cemetery is getting too full. I won't need to go to the gully again." A passing thought puckered his forehead into a frown. " Cinder doesn't like it anyhow. Nor do you."

" Well, *that*," Gip stressed, " didn't take all the time

since you was last here. What else you done? You ain't been up to no mischief, I hope? "

This time she met Christopher's gaze. He looked away first, unable to guess from her expression how much she knew.

" You've been talking to Mummy," he accused.

" Of course I been talking to your mammy," Gip acquiesced. " She says you don't love her as you used to."

Christopher flounced off the bed. But he did not leave immediately. He leant against the doorpost with his back to Gip. He seemed to be considering what he he should reply, and she did not interrupt him. A thought that raced through her head raised its own small gust of fear.

" Well, I don't," Christopher said finally. " And I'm not going to tell you why."

He ran off through the yard, leaving the door open. She called but he did not return.

In the triangular garden Christopher tried to occupy himself. There was enough to occupy his hands, but his thoughts kept returning to Gip.

It was all her fault, of course, that he had run off and left her like that. She shouldn't have taken sides with his parents. He did not want to be asked a lot of questions about what had happened yesterday. He did not know himself. As for what he had seen—he only hoped neither Best nor Oslin would tell. Certainly *he* wouldn't. The mere memory of it made him feel unclean . . . and he rubbed his forehead against his shirt sleeve as if to wipe away the picture of Maisie and Burn that waited there, quivering with the sweat in his eyelashes.

He began to whistle. It required all his concentration to keep his lips gathered into the right pout. Even so, only a very occasional sound, and always the same flat, quavering one, punctuated his efforts. He gave it up.

He would think instead of what he was going to spend the afternoon doing. Perhaps he might persuade Essie to give him some grains of rice so that he could dig paddy-fields. The rice never seemed to grow, but that was probably his own fault. He always forgot to keep the trenches filled with water. Perhaps if he dug them at the edge of the pond they wouldn't dry up so quickly. On the other hand, the cows were sure to trample the trenches down when they came down to drink.

His thoughts shied away. He had left Gip's door open! Well, it wouldn't do any harm to let a little wind and light into the room. Anyhow, he wasn't going to shut it, not yet at any rate. He stopped digging and listened. There was no sound except a couple of black-birds Miss-Betsy-Janeing one another in the mahogany tree. He might visit the orchard and collect leaf mould. On the way there he could see if Gip's door was still open.

It was. He went on down just the same. But he did not collect any leaf mould. All the usual deposits seemed to be dug out; and he felt too indifferent about the project to search for new ones. Instead he climbed up to his favourite perch in the mango tree. From there he could see the roofs of the servants' rooms and the path, on the other side of the fence, that led down to the orchard. His mother was standing under the arbour at the far end. She seemed to be looking for somebody —for him, he supposed. A kind of panic sent him

scrambling down. At the bottom of the tree he
hesitated. He did not want to meet her; and if she was
waiting for him he couldn't return the way he had come.
This, in fact, was the opportunity he had been longing
for. Gleefully he ran round to the other side of the
orchard. It was a matter of minutes to scale the
avocado, swing out along the branch, and drop lightly
on to the cliff beyond. Ignoring Best, who called out as
he raced up the slope by the cow-shed, he made for the
back yard. He arrived panting, only slowing down so
as not to frighten Gip by too breathless an entry.

She looked up, and a smile spread over her face.

" So you come back? I thought you would."

" I left the door open," he explained between gasps.

" Never mind. You come back more quickly than
you went. And for purpose I didn't get up to shut it."

Christopher propped against the bed.

" I ran all the way from . . . from the pond," he
announced proudly.

" You ain't seen your mammy then? "

" No. Does she want me? " he inquired innocently.

" Your grandpappy was here. He call in for a few
minutes on his way to Bathsheba." She checked him
with a gesture. " It too late now. I hear the car drive
out not long before you come."

Christopher let himself fall listlessly back against the
bed.

" The mistress look for you everywhere. I told her
if you weren't in the triangle you must be in the
orchard."

" She could have called out or blown the car horn,"
he complained.

" But you wouldn't have heard down by the pond,"
Gip pointed out. She caught the quick look he gave
her, and challenged. " You *was* down by the pond, I
suppose? "

" No. I was in the orchard."

" Hiding? "

" Not exactly."

" How you mean ' not exactly,' " Gip said dis-
gustedly. " Either you was hiding from you mammy
or you wasn't."

" I saw her coming and ran." The words were a
whisper.

Gip paused.

" Then it serve you right," she declared. " I don't
know what come over you, you never done nothing like
that before—and it's a most unnatural thing to do,
Master Christopher, running away from your own
mother! That's why the Lord punish you. If you had
gone to your mammy as you should have, you would
of seen your Grandpa Fraser, maybe gone with him to
Bathsheba. You is becoming a regular little two-face.
Yesterday a whole pack of lies, and today another. I
don't know where you going end up if . . ."

Christopher spun around and buried his face in the
mattress.

" Leave me alone," he shouted, pounding the bed
with his fists. " Leave me alone. Why don't you all
leave me alone."

He bit the bedclothes to muffle the sound, but each
spasm of weeping went through him like a hiccough
tearing his chest apart.

Gip waited. In the distance she heard the breakfast

gong sound. When at last Christopher was quiet she pushed a handkerchief into his hand.

" A good cry never hurt nobody," she commented.

Christopher turned his face away. Lying on one cheek, he dabbed at his eyes with the handkerchief. When he had finished he handed it back over his shoulder. He still did not move.

" You must of been saving that one up for some time," Gip commented. " You feel better now? "

He nodded, and then shook his head.

" You ain't lost your voice, I hope? Here," Gip pulled at his shoulder, " let me see your face."

He buried his face in the bedclothes whilst he searched for his own handkerchief. Blowing his nose noisily, he stood up.

Gip inspected him critically.

" That's better," she decided. " Sometimes tears wash out more than the eyes. But you better go now. Cinder done sound the gong. And wash your face under the tap before you go in," she called after him.

20

In the days that followed Christopher was even quieter than usual. He went about his small affairs with what seemed an intense concentration and, except for meals and at bedtime, was never indoors. Mary Stevens noticed it particularly. There had always been occasions during the day when he had suddenly appeared on the verandah, or wherever she happened to be, with a question or item of news too urgent to be contained for a second longer. She missed these interruptions. When she asked what kept him so busy, his answers were short to the point of curtness.

" Painting mostly."

" But you always used to paint indoors," she insisted.

" I'm painting real things now."

" Oh, I see." But she did not. " Can I look at them? "

" If you want."

He slouched off to fetch his drawing book, and without comment handed it to her.

The early paintings in the book were familiar. Most of them were imaginative scenes of things read about, whilst the last of those she knew showed the grounds at Surrey-house in a pattern of green geometric shapes.

It was a relic of his roof-top afternoon. Over the page she entered upon a new world. Where previously the touch had been light and the tones pastel and flat, there was now a brilliance of contrasting colour. The sky blazed with an orange sun and the land was heavily scored with shadows. On the second page the pond became an expanse of blue rippled in black, through which water-lilies of a violent pink thrust fat pointing fingers. She turned the remaining pages more quickly. All of them contained paintings of an equal violence. Vaguely disturbed, she handed the book back.

" You're painting in a different way," she observed.

" I," Christopher underlined the pronoun, " I like it better."

She realised that she had made none of the usual noises of approval, and added hastily, " Oh, I like it too."

" But I don't like it at all," she told Ralph Stevens later. " It's crude and angry."

" What nonsense," he exploded. " You'll be reading his tea leaves next, and interpreting his dreams."

" That's another thing," she went on, ignoring his sarcasm. " When he had a nightmare the other night and woke up screaming he didn't ask to get in our bed. When I suggested it he said no, it was only a cow."

" Well, that's nothing to worry about. It's time he got over being frightened by dreams."

She did not add that when she had related the incident to Gip, the word " cow " had made the old negress turn grey with horror.

" Mistress," she had babbled. " You don't know what it mean to dream about cows? "

Mary Stevens had suddenly felt that she did not want to know.

" Call yourself a Christian? " she had laughed, pushing the tension aside. " Surely you don't read Old Moore as well? "

Whether or not Gip believed in Old Moore, she had started to mumble her prayers almost before Mary Stevens reached the door.

Gip was not well enough to go to the beach on Sunday. As soon as he was dressed Christopher went to see if she might, at the last moment, change her mind.

" I like it better when you are there," he explained.

" You're a big boy now," Gip told him. " You don't need me no more. Only promise you won't go out of your depth."

He promised.

" But it's not the same at all," he added; then, more brightly, " Anyhow, I'll come and tell you all about it when I get back."

Gip looked away.

" Master Chris," she began. But the words stuck in her throat.

Christopher's eyes widened.

" Why, you're crying," he said. " Does it hurt a lot then? " he asked softly, running his fingers over the back of her hand.

" A little."

She put out her arms and gathered him to her. He felt her cheek wet against his as he pressed his face into the curve of her neck.

" Don't cry," he told her. " It will go away."

" Yes," she repeated. " It will go away."

For a moment they lay together. Then Gip pushed him upright by the shoulders. Her hands slid down his arms and tightened about his wrists.

" The pain gone now," she murmured.

He bent over and kissed her on the forehead, just as she did whenever he was ill and she had to leave him.

" May the Lord bless you and keep you," she said as she released him.

" I'll come and see you just as soon as I get back," he told her from the door.

" The Lord bless you, son," she repeated.

The ambulance arrived shortly before eleven o'clock.

" I should be going to service," Gip observed to Cinder and Donald as they helped her in. " This ain't no hour to be going to hospital."

She turned on Cinder.

" Don't weep, woman," she said crossly. " I ain't dead yet."

21

CHRISTOPHER FELT sure that something must be wrong. To begin with, he had kept his parents waiting in the car because his farewells to Gip had taken longer than intended; yet his father had said nothing. Then, when they reached Fairmont, he had been allowed to go off by himself instead of having to sit around with the grown-ups until breakfast was ready.

" You go outside and play," his mother had told him. " I'll call you."

This was a tremendous concession. There was a great deal to see and do at Fairmont, but he had never before been given free access to the entire property. There was, for example, a pond, much bigger than the one at Surrey-house. He had several times seen it in the distance as the car rounded the drive; but that was all. And it was a particularly interesting pond because the water was slightly brackish and quite large fish inhabited it. In addition, one bay was entirely overgrown with water hyacinth. They floated on inflated roots and pushed flower stalks high above the water. Each stalk was a cluster of mauve and blue butterflies.

Then there was the orchid house. This was built

against the drawing-room wall, but its contents had previously only been glimpsed through the glass panels of a door that was kept locked. Today, he did not know whether by chance or design, the door was ajar. He went in. In beds around a small goldfish pool were more varieties of terrestrial orchid than he had ever imagined existed. Pink, purple, and bright orange, they exploded at eye-level into shapes as strange as fireworks on Guy Fawkes's day. But the orchids that hung from the roof in wire baskets, or clung to cradles of charcoal and coconut fibre, were even more startling. Some wore long sepals that drooped below their chins like Chinamen's moustaches. Others had eyes on tall stilts and grimaced with protruding tongues. None but the wild cattleyas had any scent. Although he didn't normally like scentless flowers, in this case it hardly seemed to matter. Anyhow, it was impossible to imagine what sort of perfume such weird creatures would possess.

In contrast to this neatness and display, the lawns at Fairmont were unkempt and the garden beds ordinary. All his aunt's attentions were, he imagined, lavished on the orchids. There were, on the other hand, several very climbable trees. He was trying to decide between the ease and height of a tamarind and the slippery challenge of a Spanish ash when his mother called him for breakfast.

" As soon as you are finished you can put on your trunks," she told him, " and go down to the beach. We'll come later." And, much to Christopher's surprise, she did not add the usual string of injunctions but contented herself with a mere " Don't do anything silly or dangerous."

The tide was out and the beach deserted. Christopher debated what he should do first. Since he had only just eaten he shouldn't, perhaps, go in the water yet. There could be no harm, though, in digging a series of tunnels and channels so as to conduct the water into a hole large enough to sit in.

Having done that, he filled his trunks full of wet sand, so full that he had difficulty in rising to his feet and had to hold the trunks up at the sides so that the weight of sand would not pull them off. Then, of course, he had no alternative but to go into the sea so as to rid himself of the gritty feeling between his legs. Nobody was there to see, so he pulled his trunks off and washed out the last particles. He had never before been in the sea without trunks, and the smoothness of the water against his belly proved a most agreeable sensation. According to Gip, it was wicked to be naked—probably even under water. The fact that the negro boys in the tenantry bathed at the standpipe without any clothes at all was no argument, she had told him; it merely proved that he shouldn't.

But then, the boys in the tenantry did all kinds of things that he was not allowed to do. Those drawings on the agaves, for instance, that Cinder didn't like him to look at. . . . He knew now why she didn't.

It would be awful if a large wave came and snatched his trunks out of his hand and carried them away. He'd have to go all the way back to the house in his birthday suit. His father would be horrified—as would everybody else. He might, on the other hand, pick some of

178

those sticky leaves that grew on a creeper in the woods and plaster them over the most important parts—like Adam and Eve. But, all things considered, it was perhaps better to put his costume on again.

He lay on his back and closed his eyes. It was only possible to do this when the sea was completely calm. Otherwise the waves splashed into your face just as you were taking a breath. If there was a current, of course, you were likely to wake up miles from where you had started. He righted himself hurriedly. There was no danger. However, to be on the safe side, he pointed his head towards shore.

Propelling himself backwards with small kicks, he floated smoothly until his spine grounded on the beach.

" All hands ashore," he yelled, scrambling to his feet. " And be careful, there may be cannibals."

As a precaution he picked up a stick and poised it, ready to shoot. They advanced up the sand back into the jungle.

" Food and fresh water first," Captain Christopher Stevens announced. " Later we'll collect palm leaves and build a shelter for the night in case of animals."

It was afternoon by the time the Stevenses returned home. Cinder met the car to collect the wet bathing-suits and towels.

" Was everything all right? " Mrs. Stevens asked.

Cinder nodded. " Yes'm."

Christopher prepared to accompany Cinder.

" Chris," his mother stopped him. " I want you for a minute."

" Can't I go and see Gip first? " he asked. " I promised to go and see her as soon as I got back."

Mrs. Stevens exchanged glances with Cinder.

" You go ahead, Cinder," she told her. " I'll send Master Chris out to you later."

Christopher pouted and followed his mother indoors. She led the way into his room and sat on the edge of the bed.

" Close the door," she told him, " and come here."

Somewhat mystified, he obeyed, planting himself in front of her but just out of reach.

" Do you remember," she began, " my telling you some time ago that Gip was very ill and might not be able to work any more? "

He nodded.

" Well," her eyes moved restlessly to the window and back again. " Uncle Francis doesn't know how serious it is yet, but he has decided that Gip should go to hospital where she can be properly looked after. They may have to operate."

Christopher's eyes widened.

" You mean cut her open? " he said in an awed voice. " But how? She has rheumatism in . . . in . . . everywhere."

" It's not rheumatism. It's something much more serious."

" But when? " Christopher asked. " When are they going to do it? "

" The ambulance came this morning," his mother answered, " when we were at Fairmont . . ."

Christopher stepped back as if she had struck him.

" That's not true," he said. " She told me to come

and see her as soon as I got back. She wouldn't have said . . ." But the expression on his mother's face checked him. " It's not true," he shouted, dashing for the door. He fumbled with the handle.

" Gip," he yelled; and again, halfway down the corridor, " Gip."

Mary Stevens did not move until his cries faded in the distance and the silence eddied back around her. Wearily she stood up and crossed to the window. The sunshine poured down as usual, and the cold altar scent of ginger-lilies floated up on the waves of heat.

Afterwards she wondered what she had thought about in those few minutes.

Cinder had washed out the bathing-suits and towels. She was hanging them on the line to dry when Christopher rushed past on his way to Gip's room. His face was as white as her apron. She dropped the clothes back into the bucket and ran after him.

" Gip," she heard him yell.

He pounded on the door. It was locked. There was no answer.

" Gip." The scream turned into a sob. Then, as she reached him, his knees gave way and he fell in a heap on the ground. " Gip," he sobbed, pressing his forehead into the dust.

Cinder knelt beside him and half-lifted him on to her lap. He did not resist. She stroked the back of his head.

" There, there," she murmured. " There ain't nothing to cry about. She'll come back. They'll make her well again, you'll see. And she'll be much stronger when she comes back, much stronger." And unconsciously as she spoke she began to adopt the sing-song that Gip had used on such occasions of intimacy and grief. " The last thing she said to me was ' Tell Master Chris not to worry. I'll soon be back.' "

During the remainder of the day and throughout the next, Cinder repeated that final phrase of Gip's until she too began to believe it. For Christopher it represented all of hope, the one thing to which he could cling when the tide of remembering overwhelmed him and threatened to suck him into its dark undertow.

" Are you sure that's what she said? " he would ask.

And Cinder would reply, in mock petulance, " I done tell you so, Master Chris."

Because it was to Cinder that Gip had last spoken, he could scarcely be separated from her. Once he disappeared on some mysterious business of his own. When she found him later in the pets' cemetery and asked why he hadn't told her where he was going, he only hung his head. She guessed the reason when, later, as they gathered cowdung on the slope beyond the pond, he suddenly said, " If anything happens to her, I won't pray ever again."

She did not tell him what she thought of that remark, preferring to meet the problem when it became one. And that night, when she heard him say his prayers, she noticed that he seemed, for a change, to be listening to what he was saying.

It had been an unending day. She was glad to turn out the light and leave him.

Then it was Monday.

Christopher wished that he had been going to school. In bed the previous night he had decided that he must divest himself of his one great lie, the *Book of Games*. It stood between him and the surety that his prayers would be listened to. But there were still two weeks of holiday. The best that he could do was promise to confess the book's non-existence and to tell no more lies. He did not mind if Ronnie *did* take his place as leader. He could only do so by telling stories about babies and girls, and he, Christopher, already knew all that and didn't care any more anyhow. He would tell him so too, and if Ronnie didn't shut up, he'd just stuff his fingers in his ears in the most obvious way possible and walk off.

He practised the gesture to perfect its air of scorn, marching up and down the path in the triangular garden. Cinder asked him what he was doing but he pretended not to hear.

" Do you think," he inquired, when he had completed this divertissement, " that Macklin would give me some cement? "

" Where Macklin going get cement from? Cement cost money."

" But I only need a little."

An idea had occupied him ever since he had seen the water hyacinths in the pond at Fairmont—namely that there were no water hyacinths at Surrey-house and that he could easily convert one of his truck-tyre beds into a pool for them. It was merely a matter of digging out all the earth and packing pebbles into the bottom. Once these had been plastered over with cement he would have a suitable container, since the heavy metal rims, though rusty, were still waterproof. To prevent any objections on the part of the sanitary inspector he could take some fish out of the tank in the fernery, or from the pond, and introduce them into his own pool. They would eat the mosquito larvæ, and meantime he would have water hyacinths growing so cunningly among the other, exactly similar truck tyres that nobody would realise they were not growing in earth like anything else.

The only difficulty was the supply of cement.

" Why you don't ask your mammy? " Cinder suggested.

He thought for a moment.

" Because I don't want to," he pouted.

" Well, there ain't any other way."

In that case he would have to do without his hyacinth pond. It was a pity because it was a very good idea. He would have liked, too, to have something new to show Gip when she returned. The only thing she didn't know about was the avocado at the back of the orchard; and he couldn't show her that because it would frighten her to death.

His heart jumped.

" Do people die," he asked, " when they cut them open in hospital? "

" Not nowadays," Cinder told him, " though they mostly did in the old days. You don't remember," she laughed, " how when you was a little, little boy you used to play you was a doctor like your Uncle Francis? You had a case and three instruments—a knife to cut them open with, a fork to hold them apart, and a spoon to scoop out their insides. We was sure you'd grow up to be a doctor."

Christopher wrinkled up his nose disparagingly.

" I don't want to be a doctor any more. I shall be a painter . . . or one of those men Granddad Fraser told me about who go around the world collecting plants."

He imagined himself walking in forests where orchids, as curiously shaped as those at Fairmont but far more wonderful in colour, flamed in a green twilight. They sat in the arms of monstrous trees as though held regally out of reach of the ferns and creepers that tangled in the underbrush.

" Perhaps I could be both," he added thoughtfully. " In Africa they have water-lilies with leaves so big . . ." He held his arms apart. ". . . Bigger than that, so big that you can sit on them."

" You making it up, Master Chris," Cinder cautioned. " What Gip always telling you about making up stories? "

" It's not a story," he protested indignantly. " Granddad Fraser told me so, and he showed me a picture besides. They have turned-up edges so that the water can't get in, and the Africans use them like boats."

" I'd want to see that with my own two eyes," Cinder commented disbelievingly.

" The only trouble about Africa," he went on, ignoring her, " is that there are so many wild animals, especially snakes. . . ." He added a snake to the jungle scene he was composing. . . . " Big ones that wind themselves around the trees and hang down so as to bite you when you pass—except that the really big ones don't bite. They crush you to death and swallow you whole. Then they go to sleep for a month."

" And what you want to go to that sort of place for? " Cinder asked.

Christopher considered her with exasperation. It was no use trying to explain about the orchids. She wouldn't understand. Anyhow, there wasn't time. He had evolved a wonderful picture and intended to paint it while it was still vivid in his mind.

He was engaged in an intricate pattern of emerald and black that was his idea of a boa constrictor when Cinder announced that it was time for bed. While she grumbled impatiently he added a crimson tongue, and then trailed after her to the bathroom, his thoughts still in the jungle.

He had crossed the pond on a huge water-lily pad which was now moored to the bank. The forest began tamely enough—in fact it was just like the pet's cemetery, dark and moist, with curtains of convolvulus hanging from the limbs of trees. He pushed them aside. Beyond it was even darker. The sunlight was gathered into solid beams that dazzled more than they illuminated. Even so, it would be safer, he thought, to keep close to them, using the shafts as stepping stones through the shadows.

At first he saw little. Then, as his eyes grew accustomed to the dark, he realised that he was in a long aisle of tree trunks. It was like St. David's Cathedral . . . which was disappointing because orchids, he knew, did not grow in churches. But he was wrong. He had scarcely gone twenty yards before the avenue widened out. In a small clearing stood the largest tree he had ever seen, its entire bole covered with crimson cattleyas. They leaned sideways, hanging out their spotted tongues, or peered upwards, catching the sunlight on their wild faces. The dead ones hung like rags and the buds were pointed like candle-flames.

He looked up to see how far the pillar of flowers stretched. Hurriedly he stepped back, snatching his hand to his mouth to push back the cry that rose in his throat.

Sitting in the fork of the tree, with its great length coiled about the branch above it, was a snake of monstrous proportions. Its painted head was erect, unmoving. It seemed to be watching him.

Curiously, after the initial shock he did not feel afraid. He found himself wondering how near he dare approach the tree before its guardian would pounce. Probably it wouldn't at all. He had heard it said that these big snakes only attacked people who were naked— like Africans. They had probably learnt by experience that clothes were indigestible. He looked down to make sure that he was properly clad.

Encouraged, he stepped forward. The snake did not move. He took another pace; then another. His heart began to pound but he edged still nearer to the tree. He must be, he thought, within arm's reach of it. But he did not dare take his eyes off the snake to see. He put out a hand. As his fingers closed on an orchid the squat head he had been watching seemed suddenly to grow in size and fill his whole vision. The next moment he was caught in a tangle of dark skeins.

Sitting up, Christopher tore at the blanket wrapped

187

around his face. It came loose, and a moon, thin as the paring from a golden god's fingernail, shone full in his eyes. He blinked. Gip, of course, had not yet drawn the curtains. But it was all right. She was still there, sitting peacefully in the rocking chair. There was nothing to be afraid of.

Turning over on his face, Christopher went back to sleep.

22

There was only one car in the long procession that followed Gip's coffin to St. Paul's Church. Behind the hearse the entire tenantry walked, and behind them the Stevenses' car crawled at a pace dictated by the black-mantled horses. Donald drove, with Cinder beside him and Christopher and his mother in the back.

Although it was only two miles, to Mary Stevens the journey seemed unending. They had not yet rounded the bend that brought them to the main road; and beyond that lay all the length of St. Paul's village. She glanced at Christopher, sitting bolt upright and staring straight ahead. His face was the colour of the lilies he had piled on the coffin's head. If only she had been as strong-minded as she had originally intended! He should not have been allowed to endure this prolonged agony. It was more than any child should suffer—and she was not fooled by the fact that, so far, he had shed no tear. She knew that he was suffering more than anyone present. Gip had been as close to him as a parent—closer, she confessed. She had been the morning sunlight that fluttered behind his eyelids and woke him; she had made the colours of his day; and her life had not left his when she put out the lamp at night. She herself had sometimes resented the fact that Gip should reap an affection that was hers by rights . . . but now her eyes only burned at the thought of the finishing harvest.

She put a hand over Christopher's, lying on the seat beside her. He did not appear to notice.

For all that was dear to her she would not want to relive the last twenty-four hours. She shook her head to push away the vision of Christopher's face when, after what had seemed a lifetime of gathering her courage, she had at last told him. Life had drained from his cheeks and from his eyes, leaving a mask as cold and pallid as an idiot old age. She had expected him to tremble and collapse; but when she had put out her hands to catch him he had remained rigid under their grasp, unaware of their weight on his shoulders.

" Will they bury her at St. Paul's? " he had asked.

" Yes, this afternoon . . ." But she had been unable to add the phrase rehearsed so carefully: " It would be better if you did not go." All she had managed was: " Where are you going? " as he had turned abruptly away.

" To pick flowers."

What would she have liked? Would she have wanted him to bury his head on her shoulder and weep out the misery that steeled his voice and his body? She did not know. Perhaps he might have if she had used the right words. But what would have been the right words?

" Pick all you want," was what she had said.

She stirred herself and took her hand away from Christopher's. It was strange, too, that impassivity of

Donald and Cinder—Cinder who wept when she was complimented on a good job done, and Donald who had had tears in his eyes on her wedding day. Was everyone dead? And what had this old woman taken from them so as to leave them lifeless as herself? The hearse was piled high with flowers. There was not a patch in the tenantry, she was sure, where a rose or a geranium showed colour. There was not a single bloom left in the triangle, nor a eucharist lily or a tube-rose in all the gardens at Surrey-house. Christopher had stripped his plants to a blossomless mourning: the rarest, those that were never picked; the most fragile, those that would scarcely last till the funeral service was over. With wire he had bound them into the rough semblance of wreaths and crosses, keeping out only the lilies and tube-roses to put on Gip's face.

The procession halted at the churchyard gate. Christopher got out and joined the long queue of walkers.

Somehow he sat through the service. All the fibres in his being rebelled against what the priest was saying. If they had had mouths as uncontrollable as their sensations, a thousand would have shouted out, " No, no."

And somehow, too, he managed to walk calmly beside Donald, who was bearing the head of the coffin, to the open grave. But there was a knot of sickness in the pit of his stomach. He felt that he would soon have to take hold of it with his fingers so as to keep it from uncoiling. It had been there all day; and he must prevent it from doing what it threatened to do.

The bearers lowered the coffin. The priest scattered earth on it and the mourners cast flowers.

Suddenly Donald broke away from the group of people beside the grave. He ran between Christopher and his mother where they stood a little apart. A low moan floated out on the silence behind him.

It was coming! It was coming! The long slow spasm he had been expecting. He could not hold it; he could not keep it in any longer. It was unwinding itself. It was on him! . . .

" Gip," he screamed. " Gip."

Mary Stevens leapt forward to grasp him; but it was someone else who did, one of the bearers on the edge of the pit.

And then she had him. Then, as the high wail went up, she held him against her. And her body shook and she did not know if she was weeping for Gip or weeping because he was again the child that Gip had nursed—a child . . . for a few minutes more as he clung to her he was a child—a few minutes more that were the last of his childhood.

Caribbean
Writers
Series

GEOFFREY DRAYTON was born in Barbados in 1924. He took a degree in Political Economy at Cambridge. After university, he lived for several years in Canada, working first as a research economist with the government, and then as a schoolmaster. He returned to the UK in 1951 where he worked as a free lance journalist for a time. In 1953 he started work on the staff of *Petroleum Times* – of which he subsequently became an editor. He is at present on the staff of the Economist Intelligence Unit. He has published two other novels – *Three Meridians* (published in Toronto in 1951), and *Zohara* (published by Secker & Warburg in 1961).

An imaginative small boy leaves his childhood behind in the course of a school holiday. People puzzle Christopher. His father, an unsuccessful sugar planter, resents his own dependence on his wife's family and includes Christopher in his resentment. His mother, though she loves her husband, is also frightened of him and of losing the baby she is carrying – which is what happens. However, the central character in Christopher's life is his black nanny, Gip, through whom he comes to know the villagers with their colourful customs and superstitions. Because of a succession of experiences, only partially understood and therefore arousing unreasonable fears and ecstatic hopes, he begins to grow up and to realise that even pain and sadness are necessary stages on the road to maturity.

Cover design by Joint Graphics